Barbara Cartland

The Love Pirate

G.K. Hall & Co. • **Thorndike, Maine**

Published in 2000 by arrangement with International Book Marketing Limited.

G.K. Hall Large Print Paperback Series.

The text of this Large Print edition is unabridged.
Other aspects of the book may vary from the original edition.

Set in 16 pt. Plantin by PerfecType.

Library of Congress Cataloging-in-Publication Data

Cartland, Barbara, 1902–
  The love pirate / Barbara Cartland.
    p. cm.
  ISBN 0-7838-9265-9 (lg. print : sc : alk. paper)
  1. Malaya — Fiction. 2. Ocean travel — Fiction. 3. Large
type books. I. Title.
PR6005.A765 L656 2000
  823′.912—dc21   00-061377

Author's Note

During the reign of Vyner Brooke, the last White Rajah, he practically put down head-hunting, but when the Japanese invaded Sarawak during World War II his embargo was lifted.

When the Rajah and Ranee returned to the island after Japan was defeated, the Dyaks showed them a large collection of Japanese heads, all smoked and hanging in a special place. The warriors related gleefully how they had sent their prettiest daughters down to a pool in the jungle to bathe.

As soon as the Japanese crept up to stare at them, the Dyaks had lopped off their heads as they went by.

"Taking Japanese heads very fine sport," they laughed. "Very, very funny game!"

Chapter One

1885

"I hear you are going away again, Theydon," the Honourable D'Arcy Charington said, settling himself into the reserved compartment and lighting a cigar.

"The Prime Minister has asked me to visit the Far East, starting with Singapore," Lord Saire replied. "I am to give him a report on the general aspect of trade and how our far-famed diplomacy is doing its job."

D'Arcy Charington laughed.

"It sounds very pompous and I certainly do not envy you."

"It will be a change," Lord Saire remarked.

"You sound as if you are glad to be getting away from England. I had a feeling you were not enjoying yourself this weekend."

"It was very much the mixture as before," Lord Saire said with a note of boredom in his voice.

"Good God, Theydon! You are hard to please!" D'Arcy Charington ejaculated. "I suppose there were more beautiful women to the square yard than one would find anywhere else in the world, and the Prince certainly seemed amused."

"The Prince is always amused when there are beautiful women about," Lord Saire replied.

His friend D'Arcy Charington laughed.

"His Royal Highness really is fantastic! One sees that glint in his eye and an alert expression on his face the moment one of the beauties comes gliding into the room."

He paused, then added:

"Cynic though you may be, Theydon, you must admit they are damned beautiful."

Lord Saire also lit a cigar before he replied. Then as he extinguished the match he said slowly:

"I was thinking last night that they behave exactly as if they were goddesses sitting on the top of Mount Olympus, and we were mere mortals grovelling at the foot of it."

D'Arcy Charington looked at him speculatively.

"Of one thing I am quite certain, Theydon," he said, "you have never grovelled at the foot of anybody, however arched the instep, however attractive the little pink toes may have been."

"Really, D'Arcy, you talk like one of those French novels we used to read and chuck out the window when we were in Paris together."

"We did have fun, did we not?" D'Arcy asked. "At the same time, Theydon, French women, alluring though they may be, cannot compare with our English beauties."

"It is not always classical features and a curved body which attract a man," Lord Saire said.

"Then what else?" his friend questioned.

Lord Saire did not reply and D'Arcy Charington said:

"The whole trouble with you, Theydon, is that you are spoilt, you are too rich, too good-looking, too damned successful at everything you undertake! It is unnatural!"

Lord Saire's eyes twinkled.

"In what way?" he enquired.

"Well, you pick the ripest peaches from the tree, or rather they fall into your arms before you even lift your hand towards them, with the result that you are satiated — that is the word, old chap — you are satiated with the good things of life and just do not know when you are well off."

"Perhaps I would prefer to have to make an effort to do the picking, as you call it," Lord Saire said, "or to put it another way, I would rather do my own hunting."

D'Arcy Charington laughed.

"I thought Gertrude was running you too hard this weekend. She has always been extremely possessive, and once a man is in her clutches she never lets go."

Lord Saire did not reply, and although his friend knew that on principle he never talked about his love-affairs, he could not resist saying:

"Perhaps you are wise, Theydon, to get away while you can. I really would not relish seeing you trailing behind Gertrude's chariot wheels."

"That is something I have no intention of doing," Lord Saire said positively.

His friend smiled to himself.

He knew now why there had been a definite glint of anger in Lady Gertrude Lindley's beautiful eyes, and why Lord Saire had seemed more elusive than usual at a party which had included as the guests of the Duke of Melchester the cream of the society which circled round Marlborough House.

Those who were invited to entertain the Prince of Wales had all been women married to members of the nobility, or else widowed.

Several of the men like Lord Saire and D'Arcy Charington ostensibly were unattached, but were invited because they were discreetly paired in their hostess's mind with one of the acclaimed beauties.

Or else they were included as elusive foxes to be hunted down by females who, D'Arcy Charington had often said, wore their conquests just as Indians wore scalps of their enemies at their waists.

Looking at him now, D'Arcy Charington thought, as he had done so often before, that his friend Lord Saire was undoubtedly one of the most attractive and handsome men of his generation.

It seemed almost unfair that at the same time he should also be wealthy and extremely intelligent.

The Prime Minister, the Marquess of

Salisbury, and his predecessor Mr. Gladstone had entrusted Lord Saire with missions of importance that had never been accorded to any other man who was so young.

Officially attached to the Foreign Office, Lord Saire had an unofficial diplomatic status which sent him all over the world to make personal and usually private reports on what he saw and heard.

"When are you leaving?" D'Arcy asked when neither man had spoken for some minutes.

"The day after tomorrow," Lord Saire replied.

"So soon! Have you told Gertrude?"

"I find it advisable never to inform anybody when I am going away," Lord Saire answered. "I loathe scenes of farewell, and if I promise to write I never keep it."

He spoke with a note almost of violence in his voice, and his friend thought shrewdly that he must have avoided many scenes in the past by slipping away before some woman was aware that it was his intention.

"Well," he said, "you are off to pastures new, and perhaps I am envious. There will be little to do when the shooting is over and it's too frosty to hunt. The Prince is talking of going down to Cannes after Christmas. London will be empty."

"You might do well to join his Royal Highness."

"I could not stand a month of all that bowing and scraping," D'Arcy replied. "If I had the choice I would rather come with you."

Lord Saire smiled.

"There is nothing you would dislike more. There is not only a lot of tiresome bowing and scraping to local nabobs, but it can also be at times extremely uncomfortable. If you saw some of the places in which I have stayed you would be surprised."

"It would not be worse than the years we spent together in the Army," D'Arcy said.

"That is true," Lord Saire agreed. "I had almost forgotten the discomfort of manoeuvres and forced marches, and the inane conversation we had to listen to in the Mess."

"It was not much worse than the conversation we were forced to listen to this weekend," D'Arcy Charington said. "I thought Charlie was at his most feeble with the same old stories, the same impersonations. He amused the Prince, but no-one else."

"I am beginning to think I am too old for the whole racket," Lord Saire said.

"At thirty-one?" his friend exclaimed. "My dear Theydon, you must be sickening for something. Could it be love?"

"The answer to that is a decisive no!" Lord Saire said. "In case you mistake my meaning, let me repeat myself, D'Arcy, I am not in love and have no wish to be."

"That must be a relief to the Prime Minister," D'Arcy Charington remarked.

Lord Saire raised his eye-brows and his friend explained:

"The old boy is always in a tizzy in case he should lose you. He said to my father in the Lords the other day: 'I lose more young men through *affaires de coeur* than were ever killed on the battle-field!'"

"Your father can set the Prime Minister's mind at rest," Lord Saire said. "Love is something which does not enter into my plans, and therefore it will not interfere with the P.M.'s."

"You will have to marry sometime."

"Why?"

"Mainly because you need an heir. Someone will have to inherit that mountain of possessions."

He paused before he said reflectively:

"I often think that Saire House needs a mistress and half a dozen children to make it habitable. It is too architecturally perfect to be a home without them."

"I like it as it is," Lord Saire replied. "Besides, D'Arcy, can you imagine me with a wife?"

"Very easily! Gertrude, for instance, would look magnificent in the Saire diamonds!"

"As we are speaking off the record," Lord Saire answered, "I cannot think of anyone less suited to be my wife than Gertrude."

"You mean she is too demanding and too possessive?" D'Arcy Charington asked sympathetically.

"Yes, she is that, and as a matter of fact I doubt if she has a brain of any sort," Lord Saire answered. "She is beautiful, I grant you that, one of the most beautiful women I have ever seen, but when you have said that, you have said all."

"Good God, Theydon, what else do you want?"

"A great deal, as it happens."

"Tell me."

"Certainly not! If I did, you would find it impossible not to go round looking for the sort of creature I described to you, and if you found her you would force me up the aisle just so that you could be my best man!"

D'Arcy Charington laughed.

"All right, Theydon, have it your own way. Enjoy yourself in intellectual isolation, but I warn you, you will be very lonely in your old age sitting in all your glory at Saire without a helpmate, or whatever the expression is."

"I shall be perfectly content to enjoy the company of my friends, like you, D'Arcy, and to be Godfather to their children, of whom I have quite a number already."

"Good Lord! And I suppose you have renounced the flesh and the devil on their behalf?"

"Of course," Lord Saire agreed, "but not on my own behalf! My Godparents, who are dead by this time, certainly did nothing for me when they were alive."

"And what do you do for your Godchildren?"

"I send them a guinea for Christmas and ten guineas when they are confirmed. After that I can wash my hands of them."

"All very laudable," D'Arcy said with a mocking note in his voice. "But I would be much happier, Theydon, to see you with a son of your own and perhaps one or two pretty daughters."

"God forbid!" Lord Saire laughed. "And one of the things I am determined to avoid, D'Arcy, is other people's daughters. The Duchess was hinting quite broadly this weekend that Katherine would make me a very commendable wife."

"I hope you will not consider such a thing," D'Arcy Charington said quickly.

"Why not? I thought you wished me to be married."

"Not to one of the Duke's daughters! Can you imagine anything more ghastly than having him as a father-in-law? And anyway, from what I have seen of his offspring, they look rather like his race-horses and are as dull as ditch-water."

"What young girl is not?" Lord Saire asked. "Not that I have met many of the species."

"There must be some attractive young women about," D'Arcy Charington said. "After all, the cygnet becomes a swan and Gertrude and her like must all have been cygnets at some time."

"And doubtless as dull as ditch-water," Lord Saire said mockingly.

"Well, I shall take up the matter with you again when you return from the East," D'Arcy Charington said. "Of course you may lose your heart in the meantime to some alluring black-eyed houri — who knows?"

"As you say — who knows?" Lord Saire repeated with a faint smile on his lips.

The train was running into the terminus when D'Arcy Charington stubbed out his cigar and put his hat on his head.

"You must forgive me, Theydon, if I hurry away as soon as the train comes to a standstill. I have rather an important appointment."

"An important appointment?" Lord Saire echoed. "Male or female?"

"Male, and as it happens — my Bank Manager."

"Who of course is far more important than anyone else," Lord Saire laughed.

"In my case undoubtedly so," D'Arcy Charington replied. "I dare not tell my father the extent of my debts, and as a rule I find my Bank Manager far more sympathetic."

"Then good luck!" Lord Saire smiled. "I suppose I shall see you this evening at Marlborough House?"

"Yes, the Prince invited me and it might be rather amusing."

"Well, if it is too dull," Lord Saire suggested, "we could go on afterwards. There are some farewells I would not mind making, considering I shall be away for some months."

His friend gave him a knowing smile.

"I certainly think Madame Aspanali would welcome us with open arms, and I hear she has some new and very attractive 'soiled doves' whom she has just imported from Paris."

"In which case," Lord Saire said, "we will certainly leave Marlborough House early."

As he spoke, the train ran alongside the platform and there was the usual long line of porters waiting to attract the attention of the incoming passengers.

Both gentlemen, however, relied on their valets to collect their luggage from the carriage and their trunks from the van.

As the train came to a standstill D'Arcy Charington picked up his silver-topped Malacca cane, opened the door, and sprang out onto the platform.

"Good-bye, Theydon," he said, and disappeared into the crowd.

Lord Saire was not in a hurry.

He folded the *Financial Times*, which he had been unable to read during the journey because he was talking to his friend, then rose and put on his fur-lined overcoat with its astrakhan collar.

As he picked up his top-hat and put it at an angle on his dark head, his valet appeared at the door.

"I hope Your Lordship had a good journey."

"Quite comfortable, thank you," Lord Saire replied. "Bring the *Financial Times*, Higson. I have not yet finished reading it."

"Very good, M'Lord. The brougham will be waiting for Your Lordship. I'll bring the luggage in the landau."

"Thank you, Higson. I am going to the House of Lords. I shall be changing early because I am dining at Marlborough House."

"So I understand, M'Lord."

Lord Saire stepped out onto the platform and started to walk through the milling crowd.

The train had been full, including a number of school-girls who he noticed had got on at Oxford. They were going home for Christmas, he supposed, and looked excited and happy.

They were saying good-bye to their friends as they were herded into little groups by flustered Governesses.

A number of them were being met by their parents, their mothers draped elegantly in furs and holding sable or ermine muffs up to their faces to prevent themselves from breathing in the acid smoke being belched out by the engine.

Lord Saire had moved a little way from his railway carriage when he remembered something he should have told Higson, and he retraced his steps.

His valet was still collecting his valises and despatch-cases and a number of other pieces of hand-luggage from the rack.

D'Arcy Charington's valet was also there sorting out his master's belongings.

"Higson!" Lord Saire said from the platform.

His valet came quickly to the door of the carriage.

"Yes, M'Lord?"

"On your way, stop at the florist and send a large bouquet of lilies to Lady Gertrude Lindley. Here is a card to go with it."

"Very good, M'Lord," Higson said, taking the

18

envelope which Lord Saire handed to him.

As he turned away again Lord Saire decided that that was the last bunch of flowers Gertrude Lindley would receive from him.

As so often had happened in his love-affairs, he had known this one had come to an abrupt end.

He could not explain to himself why suddenly he became bored, and what had seemed attractive and desirable ceased to be so.

It was not that Gertrude had done anything unusual or had upset him in any way.

He had merely become aware that she no longer attracted him, and he found that many of her mannerisms which at one time had been alluring were now distinctly irritating.

He knew only too well that his friend D'Arcy would take him to task for being so fastidious — or perhaps changeable was the right word where women were concerned — but he could not help his feelings.

It was always, he thought, as if he sought the unobtainable, believing he had captured it, only to be disillusioned.

It was impossible to imagine that a woman could be more beautiful than Gertrude, and although when she swept into the room she looked like the Snow Queen, he found that in bed she was fiery and tempestuous and at times insatiable.

"What is wrong with me?" Lord Saire asked himself as he walked down the platform. "Why do I tire so easily, why does no woman in my life ever satisfy me for long?"

He knew that he could if he wished have almost any woman who took his fancy; in fact, as D'Arcy had said, they fell into his arms too easily.

He seldom sought a love-affair. It was just thrust upon him and it was the women who did the thrusting.

"Thank God I am going away," he said to himself, knowing that to extricate himself from Gertrude's arms would not be easy.

It would be quite impossible to explain to her why his feelings had changed and why she no longer interested him.

When he stepped out of the train the platform had been extremely crowded, but now most of the passengers had departed and there were only the porters trundling their piled trucks from the Guard's-van towards the exit.

There were quite a number of them, and Lord Saire was walking behind a porter whose truck was piled so high that it was impossible to see over it when suddenly there was a cry.

The porter came to an abrupt standstill so that Lord Saire almost ran into him.

Since they had both heard the cry of a woman in distress, the two men moved round the side of the truck to see lying on the ground there was a girl.

Lord Saire bent down to assist her to her feet and he realised that her hands had gone out to her ankle.

"Are you hurt?" he asked.

"Just my . . . foot," she answered. "It is . . . nothing much."

He saw in fact that her instep, which protruded beneath the hem of her skirt, was bleeding and her stocking was torn.

"I'm real sorry, Miss," the porter said from the other side of her, "I didn't see you, an' that's th' truth."

"It was not your fault," the girl answered in a soft, gentle voice. "I was looking round to see if anyone had come to meet me."

"Do you think if I assist you that you can stand up?" Lord Saire asked.

She smiled up at him and he had an impression of very large eyes in a pale face. He put his hands under her arms and lifted her gently.

She gave a tiny exclamation of pain, then as she straightened herself she said bravely:

"I will be . . . all right . . . I am sorry to be such a . . . trouble."

"I do not think any bones are broken," Lord Saire said, "but of course one never knows."

"It will be all right," the girl said determinedly, "and thank you very much for helping me."

"Do you think you can walk as far as the entrance?" Lord Saire suggested. "Perhaps you have a carriage to meet you."

"I thought Mama might have been on the platform," the girl answered, "but I am sure she has sent a carriage."

"Suppose you take my arm?" Lord Saire suggested. "It is not very far. I think it would take rather a long time to find you a wheel-chair."

"No, of course I can walk," she answered.

He offered her his arm, and leaning on it she managed to walk slowly, although obviously her foot was hurting her.

It was, as Lord Saire had said, not far to the entrance, and outside the station there were a number of carriages including his own brougham.

The girl looked up and down, then she said with a little sigh:

"I cannot see anything for me. Perhaps a porter could get me a hackney carriage."

"I will take you home," Lord Saire said.

"Oh . . . please . . . I do not wish to be a nuisance . . . and you have been so kind . . . already."

"It will be no trouble," he answered.

He led her to the door of his brougham, and the footman, very smart in a long brown livery coat and brown cockaded top-hat, held open the door.

Lord Saire helped the girl inside, then when he seated himself beside her the footman placed a sable-lined rug over their knees.

"Where do you live?" Lord Saire asked.

"Ninety-two Park Lane."

He gave the order to the footman, who shut the door and the horses started off.

"You are very kind," his passenger said in a low voice. "It was so . . . foolish of me not to notice the truck before it . . . knocked me down."

"I have a feeling you are new to London."

"I have not been here for some years."

"What about your luggage?"

"The school will arrange to have that delivered at home. It always annoys Mama when she meets me and has to wait while I get my trunk out of the Guard's-van."

"Perhaps we had better introduce ourselves," Lord Saire said. "As you have no luggage, I cannot peep at the label on it, as I might otherwise have done."

The girl smiled as he intended her to do.

"My name is Bertilla Alvinston."

"I know your mother!" Lord Saire exclaimed.

"Everybody seems to know Mama," Bertilla answered. "She is very beautiful, is she not?"

"Very!" Lord Saire agreed.

Lady Alvinston was one of the beauties he had described to D'Arcy Charington as being like the goddesses sitting on Mount Olympus.

She was dark, imperious, and very much admired by the Prince of Wales and all those who copied his taste in beauties. But Lord Saire was surprised to find that she had a daughter.

Sir George Alvinston had, he knew, conveniently died several years ago, leaving his wife, one of the undisputed beauties of Society, with a vast host of admirers.

But no-one had ever heard a whisper, so far as Lord Saire could remember, that there were any children of the marriage.

In fact no-one had suspected that Lady Alvinston was old enough to have a daughter of Bertilla's age.

Because he was curious he asked:

"You are returning home from school?"

"I have left school."

"Does that please you?"

"It has been embarrassing to stay there so long. I was much older than all the other girls."

"How much?" he enquired.

She turned her face a little way from him, as if she was shy, before she answered:

"I am eighteen and a half."

Lord Saire raised his eye-brows.

He was well aware that it was usual for girls in Society to make their début soon after they were seventeen, and certainly before they were a year older.

"I suppose your mother knows you are arriving?" he asked.

"I wrote and told her," Bertilla answered, "but sometimes Mama is so busy that she does not open my letters."

There was something pathetic and rather lost in her voice which told Lord Saire a great deal about the relationship between the beautiful Lady Alvinston and her daughter Bertilla.

"You tell me you do not usually come to London for the holidays?"

"No, I have spent most of them with my aunt in Bath. But she died three months ago, so I cannot go there."

"Well, I expect you will enjoy London," Lord Saire said, "even though a lot of people will be going away for Christmas."

"Perhaps we will go to the country," Bertilla said, a sudden lilt in her voice. "It used to be such fun when Papa was alive. I could ride and in the winter he would take me hunting, but Mama has never liked the country, she prefers to live in London."

"You will be able to ride in the Park."

"Oh, I hope so," Bertilla answered, "although it would not be as wonderful as having fields to gallop over and feeling free."

There was something in her voice which made Lord Saire look at her more closely.

He realised that while her mother was an out-standing beauty, Bertilla had a quiet loveliness which was very different.

She was small, for one thing, while it was fashionable to be tall and voluptuous.

In fact her slim figure was immature and her face had something child-like about it.

Her eyes were grey and unusually large in a face which Lord Saire, as a connoisseur of women, described to himself as "heart-shaped."

From what he could see of her hair under the unfashionable bonnet, it was very fair and curled round her forehead naturally.

Surprisingly, her eye-lashes were dark, and he thought the expression in her eyes as she looked up at him was very young and trusting.

He could not help thinking that had he been with an older woman, she would, because they were alone in the brougham, by this time be flirting with him.

She would not only flirt with every word she said but with her eyes, her lips, and every movement of her body.

But Bertilla was completely natural and was treating him as if it did not cross her mind for one moment that he was a man.

"You are not in school uniform," he said after a moment.

To his surprise, she blushed.

"I grew . . . out of it a year ago," she said after a moment. "Mama said it was not worth spending any more money, so my aunt bought in Bath what I am wearing now."

Her gown and jacket, in a sensible blue wool material with an almost indiscernible bustle, were just the sort of garments, Lord Saire thought, that an elderly aunt would choose.

While they did nothing to enhance Bertilla's appearance, they made her seem somewhat pathetic, or perhaps that impression, he decided, came from her wide eyes and her face, which was still pale after the shock of being knocked down.

"Is your foot hurting you?" he asked.

"No, it is much better, thank you. It is so very kind of you to bring me home in your carriage. Your horses are magnificent."

"I am very proud of my stable."

"And you do not use a bearing-rein?"

She looked at him anxiously as she spoke, as if she thought he might contradict her.

"Certainly not!"

She gave a little sigh.

"I am so glad. I think it is cruel. Mama says it shows off the horses and they should show off their owner."

Lord Saire was well aware that fashionable ladies insisted on bearing-reins which arched their horses' necks but could, if adjusted too tightly, be extremely painful for an animal after being used for an hour or so.

It was a cruelty that he abominated even though he knew he was very much in the minority in London where the nobility competed with one another in the smartness and luxury of their carriages.

"Do you ride in the Park?" Bertilla asked.

"Most mornings when I am in London," Lord Saire said, "but I am afraid we shall not meet, as I am going away."

"I was not thinking that," Bertilla said quickly. "I was just wondering if you knew in which part of the Park one could get away from the fashionable riders and perhaps gallop."

Lord Saire, who had thought for a moment that Bertilla was seeking to meet him again, felt amused by the knowledge that such an idea had obviously never crossed her mind.

"It is not considered 'done' to gallop in the Park," he answered. "In fact to do so in Rotten Row is decidedly a social *faux pas*. However, if you cross the bridge over the Serpentine no-one will see you."

"Thank you for telling me," she replied. "That is just what I wanted to know. But of course

Mama may not let me ride."

Lord Saire realised such a restriction would undoubtedly be very depressing, and he said comfortingly:

"I am sure she will. If I remember rightly, Lady Alvinston looks very well on a horse."

"Mama looks beautiful whatever she does," Bertilla said with what was an obvious note of admiration in her voice, "but sometimes she finds it a bore to ride and then Papa and I would go alone."

Lord Saire had the unmistakable feeling that this had been far more fun and he said in a kinder tone:

"You miss your father?"

"He was always glad to see me," Bertilla said, "and he wanted me to be with him."

The inference was obvious and Lord Saire was wondering what he could reply when he realised that his horses were drawing up outside 92 Park Lane.

"I have brought you home," he smiled, "and I hope your mother will be pleased to see you."

"I hope so too," Bertilla said. "Thank you very much for being so kind."

As a footman opened the door she added:

"I told you my name, but I never learnt yours. I would like to write and thank you."

"There is no need to do that," Lord Saire answered, "but my name is Saire — Theydon Saire!"

He got out of the carriage as he spoke and

helped Bertilla to alight.

It was a little difficult because it hurt her to stand on the leg she had injured. As the door of 92 Park Lane opened she put out her hand.

"Thank you again," she said. "I am so very, very . . . grateful."

"It has been a pleasure!" Lord Saire replied, raising his hat.

He saw Bertilla move in through the front door, then he got back into his carriage.

As the horses drove away he wondered what sort of reception the girl would get from her beautiful mother.

He felt, somehow, that since she had not been met at the station there would be no welcome for her at 92 Park Lane.

In the Hall, Bertilla smiled at the old Butler whom she had known ever since she was a child.

"How are you, Maidstone?" she asked.

"Glad to see you, Miss Bertilla, but you're not expected."

"Not expected?" Bertilla cried. "Then Mama could not have received my letter. She must know that schools break up for the Christmas holidays, and of course I could not go to Aunt Margaret's."

"No, of course not, Miss, but I've a feeling Her Ladyship didn't get your letter. She said nothing to us."

"Oh, dear!" Bertilla said. "Then I had better go up and see her. She is awake?"

She knew her mother seldom rose before luncheon-time and it was in fact only just after twelve o'clock.

"Her Ladyship was called an hour ago, Miss Bertilla, but she will be surprised to see you."

There was a warning note in Maidstone's voice which Bertilla recognised and her eyes were apprehensive as she went slowly up the stairs.

The house had had a great deal done to it, she thought, since she was last here in her father's time.

The carpet was new, the walls had been re-decorated, and there were great vases of hot-house flowers in the Hall and on the landing, an extravagance which her father would have deprecated.

As she passed the doors of the double Drawing-Room and climbed to the second floor Bertilla's feet seemed to move more slowly and her injured foot to hurt her more with every step she took.

She was also aware that her heart was beating quickly, and she told herself it was stupid to be so frightened of her mother; but then she always had been.

She knew, too, that her hand was trembling as she raised it to knock on the bed-room door and she wished she were back at school with tomorrow just another day of lessons.

"Come in!" Lady Alvinston's voice was sharp.

Bertilla opened the door slowly.

As she had expected, her mother was sitting up

in bed against a pile of lace-edged pillows. An ermine rug covered her and she was wearing a confection of pink chiffon and lace which was a perfect foil for her dark hair and white skin.

She was reading a letter and there was a pile of other letters on the bed beside her. As Bertilla came into the room, she finished the page she was reading before she looked up.

When she saw who stood there Lady Alvinston gave a little start before she said with an unmistakable note of irritation in her voice:

"Oh, it is you. I thought you were arriving tomorrow."

"No, today, Mama. I did tell you in my letter."

"I mislaid it somewhere, and I have such a lot to do."

"Yes, of course, Mama."

Bertilla drew nearer to the bed and Lady Alvinston asked:

"Why are you limping?"

"I was knocked down on the platform," Bertilla replied. "It was stupid of me. I did not notice a truck coming behind me with a lot of luggage."

"It is just like you to be so careless!" Lady Alvinston retorted. "I hope you did not make a scene?"

"No, of course not, Mama. A very kind gentleman picked me up and brought me home in his brougham."

"A gentleman?" Lady Alvinston's voice was shrill.

"Yes, Mama."

"Who was he?"

"He said his name was Saire . . . Theydon Saire."

"Lord Saire! Good Heavens! How could I imagine you would come in contact with him?"

There was no mistaking the anger in Lady Alvinston's eyes and Bertilla said quickly:

"I am sorry, Mama, I could not help it, and you had not sent a carriage for me."

"I have told you, I thought you were coming tomorrow. It is extremely unfortunate that you should have met Lord Saire."

"Why?"

Lady Alvinston turned her head to look at her daughter and her eyes rested on the child-like face, the fair hair under the dull, unfashionable bonnet surmounting it.

"Did you tell him who you were?"

"He asked my name and said he knew you."

"Damn!"

The swear-word seemed to ring out and Bertilla's eyes widened in astonishment.

"Mama!" she exclaimed involuntarily.

"It is enough to make anyone swear," Lady Alvinston retorted. "Could you not have realised, you little fool, that I did not want anyone, especially Lord Saire, to know I had a daughter?"

Bertilla did not speak and Lady Alvinston went on:

"He will tell Gertrude Lindley and she will be delighted to tell the whole world! She has always been jealous of me."

"I am sorry, Mama. I did not know you had no wish to own me."

"For goodness' sake!" Lady Alvinston exclaimed. "You must have the sense to know that I cannot acknowledge I am the mother of an eighteen-year-old daughter. I admit to thirty, if anyone is so ill-mannered as to ask me my age, but I do not intend to be any older."

"I am . . . sorry, Mama," Bertilla said again.

"I might have guessed you would make a mess of it," Lady Alvinston said. "You always were stupid. If you had had any brains at all in your head you would either have not told him your name or invented something."

"If only you had . . . told me that was what you . . . wanted me to do," Bertilla said miserably.

"Quite frankly, I never thought you were likely to encounter any of my friends," Lady Alvinston said, "and I have made arrangements so that they should not meet you."

Bertilla did not speak and Lady Alvinston said suddenly:

"And what do you mean by driving alone with Lord Saire in his brougham? Surely you realise that, if there was nothing to meet you, you should have taken a hackney carriage?"

"I did suggest it," Bertilla answered, "but he said he would take me home and he had been so kind after I hurt my foot."

"I am sure he would not have offered to do that if he had thought you were grown up," Lady

Alvinston said as if speaking to herself. "He must have thought you were only a child. You do not look eighteen."

Bertilla had an uncomfortable remembrance of Lord Saire asking her age, and she recalled that she had told him the truth, but because she was so frightened of her mother she kept silent.

She would not have lied if her mother had asked her if she had told Lord Saire her age.

But she had learnt long ago when she was only a little girl that it was unwise to volunteer information, because Lady Alvinston was unpredictable and it invariably turned out to be something that should not have been said.

"Let me see . . ." Lady Alvinston went on as if she were talking to herself, "if you had been born when I was seventeen that would make you . . . fourteen if I am . . . thirty-one."

She regarded her daughter with critical eyes.

"You could easily pass for fourteen," she said, you are so small and insignificant. If anybody asks me, that is what I will say you are."

She picked up a letter which lay on the bed and said:

"Now that is settled, and after all you will not be here for long. So all you have to do is keep out of sight."

"Am I going away, Mama?"

"The day after tomorrow," Lady Alvinston replied. "You are going to stay with your Aunt Agatha, your father's elder sister."

Bertilla looked puzzled.

"Aunt Agatha? I thought that she . . ."

"Agatha is a Missionary, as you well know, Bertilla, and I have decided that you should dedicate yourself to the same cause."

"Do you . . . mean that you . . . want me to be a . . . Missionary . . . too?" Bertilla asked in a voice that shook.

"Why not?" Lady Alvinston asked. "I am sure it is a very commendable career for any girl, and, as you know, your Aunt Agatha is living in Sarawak."

Bertilla made a little muffled sound of dismay and Lady Alvinston continued:

"I wrote to Agatha when Margaret died and told her that when you left school I would send you to live with her."

"And she . . . said she would . . . have me?"

"There has not been enough time for me to have a reply, but I know she will be delighted to see you."

"How can . . . you be sure of . . . that, Mama?"

Lady Alvinston did not reply and after a moment Bertilla asked:

"When did you last . . . hear from Aunt Agatha?"

"How can I be expected to remember every letter I receive?" Lady Alvinston replied angrily. "Agatha always wrote to your father for Christmas."

"But Papa has been . . . dead for three years."

Lady Alvinston looked at her daughter's anxious face and troubled eyes, and her expression hardened.

"Will you stop making difficulties!" she said fiercely.

"But . . . Mama . . ."

"I do not intend to listen to any arguments," Lady Alvinston snapped. "There is nowhere else you can go now that your Aunt Margaret is dead."

She paused to add:

"Most girls would think themselves very lucky to see the world. You should find it very interesting, and I have always been told that travel broadens the mind."

"Am I to stay in . . . Sarawak for . . . ever, Mama?"

"There will certainly not be enough money for you to make the return journey," Lady Alvinston replied. "It is extremely expensive to send you all that way, and I suppose you will want some clothes, but not many. No-one would expect you to be fashionably dressed when there is no-one to see you but a lot of natives."

Bertilla clasped her hands together.

"Please, Mama, I do not wish to . . . live with Aunt Agatha. I remember being . . . frightened of her when I was a little girl, and Papa always said she was . . . fanatical."

"Your father said a lot of silly things to which you would have been wise to pay no attention," Lady Alvinston retorted. "You will go to your aunt, Bertilla, whether you like it or not. I do not want you here."

"Surely one of Papa's . . . cousins could . . .

have me?" Bertilla suggested desperately.

"Everybody who might accept you lives in London, and as I have just said, I do not intend you to be here," Lady Alvinston said. "Get it into your head, Bertilla, that I have no wish to be hampered by a grown-up daughter."

As she spoke, she turned her face towards the mirror on her dressing-table, in which she could see herself reflected.

She looked with satisfaction at the darkness of her hair and the whiteness of her skin against the pink of her dressing-jacket. Then she said:

"You are old enough to understand that I hope one day to marry again; but nothing, Bertilla, could put a man off more than to find himself saddled with the children of a previous marriage."

"I can . . . understand that, Mama," Bertilla replied, "but please do not send me . . . away from . . . England. Could I not go to the country? No-one would know I was there and the old servants could look after me."

"It would not be at all convenient," Lady Alvinston answered. "I intend to open Alvinston Park this summer. Everyone gives weekend parties in the country and there are certain friends I would like to entertain."

She gave a little sigh before she added:

"That is, if I can afford it."

"Then could I not go somewhere . . . else, Mama? I would not . . . cost you . . . very much."

"The answer is no, Bertilla, and I do not

intend to discuss it," Lady Alvinston said firmly. "I have managed to find enough money one way or another to send you out to Sarawak and that is where you are to go, and where you are to stay!"

"But . . . Mama . . ."

"Go away and leave me alone!" Lady Alvinston shouted. "You had better start packing what things you have. I will arrange for Dawkins to go shopping with you this afternoon, as I imagine you have no summer dresses. It will be hot in Sarawak but you are not to buy anything expensive."

As she spoke, Lady Alvinston rang a bell which stood on the table by her bed-side.

The door opened almost immediately and her lady's-maid, a gaunt-faced elderly woman, came into the room.

"Here is Miss Bertilla, Dawkins," Lady Alvinston said, "and she has come home on the wrong day, which is just what we might have expected. But at least it gives you two afternoons in which to get her all she requires."

"I'll do my best, M'Lady," Dawkins replied, "but you knows as well as I do we'll not find summer clothes in the shops at this time of the year."

"Do the best you can and do not spend too much money."

Lady Alvinston's tone was decisive and as she picked up her letters again Bertilla knew she was dismissed.

She went from the room and found her way to the small bed-room she had occupied in the past, which was on the same floor, but found it full of large wardrobes which contained her mother's clothes.

With some difficulty she discovered that she was to sleep on the top floor in a room adjoining those used by the maid-servants.

It did not upset her any more than the interview with her mother had already done, because, she told herself, it was the treatment she might have expected.

She had always known that her mother did not love her and in some way always seemed to resent her very existence.

As she sat down forlornly on the bed she told herself that she might have expected to be sent away into obscurity.

Bertilla would have been very unintelligent, which actually she was not, if she had not realised that ever since her father's death she had been nothing more than an encumbrance.

She had spent her holidays with her aunt at Bath, and her mother never wrote to her at school.

Clothes were never provided for her except when the Headmistress wrote to say quite firmly that she required certain articles of the school uniform and that it was essential that she should be provided with new books or school equipment.

Bertilla thought now that her mother could

not have found a place farther away or disposed of her more effectively.

She remembered her Aunt Agatha as a hard, forbidding-looking woman whom her father had never liked and who had obviously frightened her younger sister, Margaret, when they had been girls together.

Aunt Margaret had once told Bertilla that when she was young she had had the chance of marrying, but Agatha had prevented it.

"She thought I was too frivolous, Bertilla," she said with a little laugh. "Agatha despises worldly goods and worldly thoughts. She was always praying, and used to get furious with me when I wanted to dance."

Bertilla felt herself shiver.

What sort of life would she have with her aunt?

She knew that once she reached Sarawak there would be no escape!

Chapter Two

"It is no use, Dawkins," Bertilla said as they came out of the fifth shop in which they had tried to find suitable gowns.

"I told Her Ladyship there wouldn't be anything to be bought at this time of the year," Dawkins said sharply.

She was, as Bertilla knew, getting tired, and as a result she became more irritable with the saleswomen every time they were unable to find what Bertilla required.

It was not the fault of the girls who in the big shops were always underpaid and invariably at this time of the year were overworked by the rush of customers.

They did their best, but it was impossible in London in December to find thin gowns suitable for the tropics.

Bertilla anyway was too small for the majority of gowns which were designed for tall women who could carry a bustle with grace and dignity.

"The only thing we can do, Dawkins," Bertilla

said in her soft voice as they walked along the crowded pavement, "is to buy the material and I will make myself some dresses during the voyage."

She sighed and added:

"I shall have plenty of time."

She had lain awake all night after her mother had told her she was to go to Sarawak, feeling desperately that she would never be able to cope by herself on the journey.

She had been abroad once with her father and she had travelled with him to Scotland, but she had never contemplated looking after herself on a journey that would take her half across the world.

In ordinary circumstances, she thought, it would be rather a thrilling adventure, not going alone, but travelling with someone like her father, whom she had loved.

But to know that at the end of the long days at sea she would find her Aunt Agatha was like walking into a nightmare knowing one would be unable to wake up.

The more she thought of what her life would be like solely in her Aunt Agatha's company, and having to pretend that she wished to become a Missionary, the more she felt like running away and hiding herself in some place where her mother would never be able to find her.

But she knew that such an idea was hopeless; she had no money, for one thing, and she was quite unfitted to earn her own living.

She looked at the shop-girls as they were attending to her and thought that many of them looked thin and under-nourished, and had lines under their eyes and bad complexions.

She was sure that this was the result of the un-healthy life they led and the fact that, as she had heard and read in the newspapers, they were very poorly paid.

Because her father had been interested in current affairs, Bertilla had tried while at school to keep up with the subjects that had interested him and the events that were taking place all over the world.

In this she was very different from the majority of her class-mates, who were interested in only one thing, and that was in getting married.

As soon as they were within sight of leaving school and being launched on the Social World, their conversation was entirely of men and how to attract them.

They would giggle for hours with one another over some episode which had taken place in the holidays, or over a man they had seen when they were walking from the school demurely in a crocodile.

Bertilla found this extremely boring.

She supposed she would get married one day, but in the meantime there were so many more interesting things to read about and, if she had the opportunity, to talk about, than some hypothetical man whom she found impossible to contemplate as a husband.

She was well aware, even before her mother had told her so, that Lady Alvinston intended to remarry.

Almost before she was out of mourning the servants had gossiped about her admirers in Bertilla's hearing.

Her Aunt Margaret had been insatiably curious about the parties Lady Alvinston attended and the reports of them in the magazines and newspapers.

"Your mother is so beautiful, dear," she said to Bertilla, "one could hardly expect her to stay single and faithful to your father's memory."

"No, of course not," Bertilla had said.

At the same time, she could not help feeling that she was being disloyal to her father in agreeing so easily that her mother should have another husband.

But she had realised a long time ago, when she was still quite small, that while her father adored her mother and was extremely proud of her, there were many other interests to occupy and amuse Lady Alvinston.

It was not only Sir George's placid acceptance of the fact that he and Bertilla should be in the country while his wife stayed in London which made Bertilla aware that their lives ran on separate lines.

It was also the little hints that were dropped, many of them with deliberate unkindness, by guests who came to Alvinston Park when her mother was not there.

"Is Millicent still in London?" they would say with raised eye-brows. "Of course, she never liked the country, but you must be so glad, dear George, that the Duke is there to look after her."

If it was not the Duke, it would be Lord Rowland, Lord Hampden, Sir Edward, or any number of other names which meant nothing to Bertilla except that they were frequently mentioned in the Court Circular.

Although she accepted that her mother's beauty attracted a great number of admirers and that finally she would choose one of the most suitable of them to be her stepfather, Bertilla had not expected that this would mean her expulsion not only from her mother's side but also from England itself.

"How can I bear it?" she had asked in the darkness of the night.

Now, walking down Regent Street with Dawkins, she felt she must look at everything about her, even the passersby, carefully and searchingly because soon they would only be a memory.

Finally they arrived back in Park Lane with some rolls of muslin, cheap silk for linings, and cottons and silks for accessories to match the gowns which Bertilla must make for herself.

"Thank you very much for helping me, Dawkins," Bertilla said in her soft voice as they walked up the stairs carrying their parcels.

"I'll tell you what I'll do, Miss Bertilla," Dawkins said, suddenly gracious now that she was home and there was a cup of strong tea waiting for her, "I'll sort out some bits and pieces which her Ladyship has no further use for. There's waistbands, ribbons, and some pretty trimmings which I am sure would come in useful."

"That is very kind of you, Dawkins," Bertilla smiled.

Her mother was out, and when she had taken off her coat and bonnet she went downstairs to the Sitting-Room at the back of the house where they usually sat when they were not entertaining.

There was a portrait of her father over the mantelpiece and Bertilla stared up at his kind, intelligent face, wishing as she had wished a thousand times before that he were still alive.

"What shall I do, Papa?" she asked. "How can I live with Aunt Agatha? Sarawak is so far . . . so very . . . far away."

She waited almost as if he might answer her, then told herself that the one thing he would expect was that she should be brave.

She would never have shown him that she was afraid in the hunting field, and while this was far more terrifying than jumping a high hedge, she must not be anything but courageous about it.

"I will try, Papa," she said at length with a sigh, "but it is going to be difficult . . . very . . . very difficult."

She went to the book-case to find some books to take with her to read on the journey, hoping there might be something about the part of the world where she was being sent.

But apart from a slim biography of Sir Stafford Raffles, who had built up Singapore, there was nothing else and she wondered if she would have time to go to Mudies Library in Mount Street and see what she could find there.

She wished she had thought of it when she was out with Dawkins, but it was really too late to ask her now: she would be sitting down having her tea and would deeply resent being dragged out again.

"Perhaps there will be books on board ship," Bertilla told herself.

She felt a sinking feeling inside her at the thought of starting off on a long voyage without anyone she knew and with no-one to help or advise her.

She could not help thinking it was extraordinary that her mother should in fact send her without a Chaperon.

Then she told herself that she supposed Missionaries were a law unto themselves, and, rather like Nuns, could go anywhere in the world unprotected without getting into any difficulties.

It was all rather hard to sort out in her mind and she was just taking several more books from the shelf, intending to carry them upstairs, when Lady Alvinston came into the room.

Bertilla turned round with a smile to greet her mother, then at the expression on her face looked apprehensively at her.

Dressed in a fur-trimmed jacket with diamonds glittering in her ears and a hat ornamented with crimson ostrich-feathers, Lady Alvinston looked very beautiful.

But there was a frown on her smooth brow and her eyes were dark with anger as she looked at her daughter.

"How dare you," she said, her voice resonant with fury, "how dare you tell Lord Saire your age!"

Bertilla started and the colour drained away from her face.

"H-he . . . asked me," she stammered.

"And you were such a half-witted little fool as to tell him the truth," Lady Alvinston replied furiously.

She pulled off her long kid gloves as she said in a voice that was almost vicious:

"I might have known that to bring you here even for two nights was to court trouble. The sooner you are out of this country and out from under my feet, the better I shall be pleased!"

"I . . . I am sorry, Mama."

"And so you should be! Can you imagine what I felt when Lord Saire asked me how you were and enquired whether I was presenting you at Court this spring!"

Lady Alvinston pulled off one glove and started to undo the six pearl buttons on the other.

"Fortunately, unlike you, I am quick-witted. 'Present Bertilla?' I exclaimed. 'Whatever put such an idea into your head, My Lord? She is much too young!'

"He looked at me searchingly, as if he half-suspected I was not telling the truth. 'She told me she was eighteen and had left school,' he said. I managed to laugh, although I felt like throttling you!

"'You could not have really looked at her if you believed that, my dear Lord Saire,' I replied. 'Girls love to be thought older than they are, and actually Bertilla is only fourteen.'

"He looked surprised and I went on: 'If she had told you the truth — but I am afraid my little daughter is a very accomplished liar — she would have informed you that she has been very naughty at school and has been expelled.'"

"Oh, Mama, why did you say that?" Bertilla expostulated.

"I had to say the first thing that came into my head," Lady Alvinston snapped, "and to erase from his mind the idea that you are eighteen. Eighteen! That would make me well over thirty-six, and everybody believes that I am much younger."

Bertilla knew that actually her mother was thirty-eight, but she said nothing, and after a moment Lady Alvinston went on in a quieter tone:

"I think I convinced him! After all, you are very small, and that idiotic, child-like face of yours, which mirrors your even more idiotic mind, certainly appears immature. The sooner you are out of my sight, the better!"

She threw her gloves down on the sofa before she said:

"If anyone calls unexpectedly to see me this evening, stay in your bed-room and do not come out! You have made enough mischief already."

"I did not . . . mean to, Mama. I did not . . . know you did not . . . wish to acknowledge me as your . . . daughter."

"Well, you know now!" Lady Alvinston said, and walked out of the room.

The tears gathered in Bertilla's eyes and she stood irresolute, looking at the door that had closed behind her mother.

She had always felt unwanted ever since her father had died, but she had not realised that her mother positively disliked her.

"You will be very pretty when you are grown up, my dear," her father had said to her once, "but thank goodness as you are such a different type from your mother there need be no rivalry between you."

Bertilla had at the time been surprised that he should imply that there could ever be such a thing.

"I am certain that I could not rival anyone as beautiful as my mother," she had said to herself.

And surely it was absurd to think there could ever be such a thing as competition between a mother and her daughter.

Now she knew instinctively that her mother's irritation was not only because of her age, but because her father's prophecy had come true.

She was in fact pretty, or, as several of the girls at school had told her, lovely.

"When my brother took me out last Sunday," one of them had said to Bertilla, "he saw you and said you were the loveliest thing he had seen in a month of Sundays, let alone in a place like this."

Bertilla had laughed, but she had been pleased and flattered.

'I would not want Mama to be ashamed of me,' she had thought ingenuously. 'I have often heard her say in the past how sorry she was for people like her friend the Duchess having such plain daughters to present.'

Even her mother's indifference in not writing to her at school, not seeing her in the holidays, and not telling her of any plans for the future had not prepared her for the fact that she was to be exiled from all that remained of her family.

"With the exception of Aunt Agatha!" Bertilla whispered, and felt herself shiver.

It was raining, the sky was dark and dismal, the quay-side wet, and what could be seen of the sea was turbulent as Bertilla went aboard the P. & O. steamer *Coromandel*, which was to carry her away from England.

With its black hull and high superstructure, the look-out alert on its flying bridge and the Red Ensign fluttering at the stern, it was an impressive if not a large vessel.

All the ships which were the life-line of the British Empire and carried every year 200,000 passengers and as many merchant sea-men were smaller than 8,000 tons.

But a thousand new ships were being launched almost every year, and the great Shipping Lines, the Peninsula and Oriental, the Elder Dempster, the British India, who all based their fortunes on the Empire trade, were considering building bigger and better ships as they competed with one another.

The Shipping Lines were intensely proud of their ships and advertised them extravagantly. The *Coromandel* was a steamer with a trace of sail about her, having four tall masts and complicated rigging.

But what with the rain and feeling very small and very alone, Bertilla was concerned at the moment only with finding her cabin.

All the way down in the train she had thought that during the voyage she would at least be able to read and sew, and if no-one spoke to her over the long weeks she must just get used to her own company.

She was trying to be brave and it had been hard to say good-bye to old Maidstone and not cry when he had wished her "God-speed."

Even Dawkins had seemed like a close friend who would leave a gap in her life because she would never see her again.

She had not been surprised to learn that she was not to say good-bye to her mother: she had to leave the house at eight-thirty A.M. and Lady Alvinston had left strict instructions that she was not to be called.

"Her Ladyship didn't get in 'til after two

o'clock last night," Dawkins said.

Then, as if she thought she could salve Bertilla's hurt feelings with an explanation, she went on:

"Dead tired, Her Ladyship was, and none too pleased that some clumsy gentleman on the dance-floor had torn the frill on the skirt of her new gown. But there, I always says that dancing was only invented to give a wretched lady's-maid more work!"

Bertilla tried to smile and failed.

"Did Mama leave a message for me, Dawkins?"

"I know Her Ladyship will want you to take care of yourself, and have a good time, Miss Bertilla," she replied, which was not the answer Bertilla wished to hear.

Maidstone had her ticket, her passport, and some money ready, and a footman was sitting on the box of the carriage with instructions to see her trunks into the Guard's-van and find her a comfortable seat on the train.

It was only when she looked at her ticket that Bertilla found she was travelling not First Class, as she had expected, but Second.

This surprised her because she knew that neither her father nor her mother would have contemplated going anywhere either by train or ship without booking the best and most comfortable accommodation.

She knew that her mother resented having to spend money on her and she told herself that she might think herself fortunate she was not in fact going Steerage.

Because there was not only the rain but also a strong wind, Bertilla hurried as quickly as she could up the gang-plank of the *Coromandel* and found herself waiting with a number of other passengers to be told the number of her cabin.

The Second Class passengers were herded up one gangway and along the quay, while another was reserved for those exalted beings who travelled First Class.

Bertilla noticed that her fellow-passengers on the Second Class deck were predominantly foreigners.

She thought how colourful they looked and tried to guess from where they came.

Was the hugely fat man who looked like a Gulli from Kuala Lumpur, the dry-faced lawyer from Saigon, and the small slant-eyed man from Sumatra or perhaps Borneo?

There were a number of Chinese, who must, Bertilla thought, be returning to Singapore, where she knew there was a large community of them.

Most of them appeared to be very prosperous, but she saw on closer inspection that there were a number of sunburnt Europeans who she thought must be planters.

One thing she had brought with her was an atlas, and she hoped that on board there might be something as helpful as a guide-book.

She had always been interested in other races, and now as she looked round her she thought that if nothing else there would certainly be new people to study, and perhaps she could learn a little of their customs and history.

She was looking at an Indian woman with a beautiful scarlet sari draped over her dark hair and hiding her face, when she saw a man staring at her. His expression made her feel somewhat embarrassed.

He had golden skin and dark hair and for a moment she found it hard to place him. Then she thought that he had a combination of Dutch and Javanese features.

She had heard that the Dutch planters in the East often married Javanese girls.

With a sense of triumph she told herself that she was quite certain that she had guessed this particular man's nationality correctly, and yet it would be hard to verify if she was right.

Then because he was still staring at her she felt the colour rise in her cheeks and she looked away, glad at that moment to be able to attract the Purser's attention.

"Miss Bertilla Alvinston?" he questioned. "Oh, yes, Miss, you are in cabin thirty-seven, a single cabin to yourself. A steward will take you there."

A steward came forward to take Bertilla's small valise which she carried with her and to lead her along a narrow, low-ceilinged passageway.

"I have other luggage on the train," Bertilla said.

"It'll all be brought aboard, Miss," the steward replied.

He opened a door.

"Here's your cabin, Miss, and I hopes you find everything you require."

The cabin seemed to Bertilla to be little bigger than a very small cupboard.

She remembered that Charles Dickens on going aboard a ship for the first time in 1842 had called his cabin "a profoundly preposterous box."

But Bertilla was too thankful not to have to share a cabin with some strange woman to be critical.

There was just room for a bed and a fitted chest-of-drawers, while a curtain covered one corner behind which she could hang her clothes, and there was a wash-basin.

This could be swung down over what was supposed to be a dressing-table. After use it had to be tipped up again to send the water cascading down into a waste-tank.

It was certainly not the luxury that she had been led to expect on the *Coromandel* in the brochure she had read coming down from London in the boat-train.

But she supposed that the pictures of the Dining-Salon with arm-chairs and potted palms doubtless referred to the First Class, as did the huge, comfortable Lounge, the organ in the Picture-Gallery, and the Writing- and Card-Rooms.

"Never mind," she told herself, "at least I can be alone here."

She could not however escape the feeling that her cabin was rather like a cell allotted to a prisoner being transported to another part of the world whether she liked it or not.

Because the idea was so depressing she thought she would go up on deck and watch the ship leave.

She had always been told it was a gay and encouraging sight, with a Band playing, streamers being thrown from the quay towards the passengers, and cheers from the watching crowd as the ship set off on its long voyage.

But when she came out on deck Bertilla found there were few people prepared to brave the stormy weather to wave their good-byes.

Those bustling about on the quay-side were mostly porters still bringing trunks and cargo aboard.

There were some last-minute passengers climbing the First Class gangway who had obviously delayed their arrival until the hurly-burly of the first arrivals had subsided.

There were several ladies, Bertilla noticed, wrapped in furs and carrying umbrellas, who seemed as elegantly gowned and, at a quick glance, almost as distinguished as her mother looked when she was travelling.

They were with gentlemen in tartan overcoats with long caps attached or bowler hats on their heads, which because of the wind they had to hold firmly in place with one gloved hand.

There were also a few children in the charge of

uniformed Nannies.

Then just as the gangway was about to be re-moved Bertilla saw sauntering with noticeable dignity along the quay-side someone she recognised.

She felt her heart give a leap of excitement.

There was no mistaking the broad shoulders and handsome features of the man who had be-friended her at the station and taken her home in his brougham.

"It is Lord Saire!" she said to herself. "And he is to be aboard the *Coromandel*!"

She watched him walk up the gangway, then disappear onto the First Class deck above her.

"I shall never meet him, or even see him."

At the same time, she could not help feeling a sudden glow of satisfaction that there was at least one person on board whom she had seen before, whose name she knew, and who came from the world to which she belonged.

The fact that Lord Saire was there seemed to lighten the tightness within her breast.

The feeling of emptiness that she had experienced ever since the train carried her away from London, utterly and completely alone, was not so intense.

The gangways were pulled away from the ship's side, and now very faintly, because it was playing under cover, she could hear the strains of a Band.

There were just a few people standing below on the quay-side to wave good-bye, but they kept out of the rain and the *Coromandel* moved off smoothly without any commotion and without the dramatic effect of fond farewells.

The wind coming from the sea was cold, the rain was beating down, and Bertilla felt herself shiver.

Yet at the same time she did not feel so despairingly alone as she had expected.

It was because, although it seemed absurd, Lord Saire was aboard and he had been kind to her, very kind, when she had been in trouble.

Lord Saire, as it happened, was surveying his cabin and adjacent private Sitting-Room with a sigh of relief.

He had got away from London without Lady Gertrude being aware that he was leaving, and he had avoided what he knew would have been an uncomfortable and dramatic scene.

He told himself as he had done before that he had become far too involved.

What he had intended to be a light, frothy affair, a game played by two people who knew and understood the rules, had in fact become far too serious.

It was something which Lord Saire had never meant to happen, but it was what inevitably occurred in his love-affairs, and made him, as events repeated and rerepeated themselves almost monotonously, more cynical than he was before.

"I love you, Theydon! I love you madly,

desperately! Tell me that you will love me forever and that we will never lose this enchantment, this heavenly happiness."

It was the sort of thing that every woman said to him after he had made love to her for a short time, and he knew, just as if they had raised a danger signal, exactly what it meant.

They wanted to tie him down, they wanted to make sure that they possessed him and he could not escape.

Most of all, where it was possible, as in the case of Gertrude Lindley, they wanted marriage.

"Damn it all!" Lord Saire had said often enough to himself, "surely one can make love to a woman without having to make it a life sentence?"

But in his case it seemed as if that was almost impossible to avoid even with the women who were already married.

There was always in the insistence of their kisses the suggestion that their love should be eternal and that he should dedicate himself to them for all time.

As Lord Saire had told his friend D'Arcy Charington, he had no intention of getting married.

He found that the freedom he enjoyed as a bachelor was an ideal existence which at the moment he did not contemplate relinquishing without a struggle.

But Gertrude Lindley had been very persistent.

She had seemed to twine silken cords round him which he had begun to feel were strangling him and might, if he was not careful, become unbreakable.

She had even involved the Prince in her plotting to get Lord Saire to propose marriage.

"Only you, Sire," she had said, looking at the Heir to the Throne with her velvet dark eyes, "will understand how desperately in love I am and how different it is from anything I have ever felt before."

She had gone on to beg his assistance, and, as the Prince always liked to help beautiful women, she finally coaxed him into speaking to Lord Saire.

"I think you are being rather cruel to that pretty creature, Saire," the Prince had said in his deep voice after dinner at Marlborough House.

"Which one, Sire?" Lord Saire had enquired.

He was well aware as soon as his Royal Highness started to speak what he was about to hear.

The Prince had chuckled.

"That is the sort of answer I like to give myself, my boy! You know as well as I do that I am speaking of Lady Gertrude."

"She always assures me that I make her very happy, Sire," Lord Saire said blandly.

"So you should!" the Prince exclaimed. "You are a fine figure of a man, Saire, and a damned good lover, from all I hear!"

"I cannot profess to emulate Your Royal

Highness on that score," Lord Saire had replied, "but shall I say modestly that I do my best?"

The Prince had laughed until it turned into a fit of coughing. Then after he had sipped his brandy he said:

"Confidentially, Saire, what are you going to do about her?"

"Nothing. Sire, that I have not done already."

For the moment the Prince had looked non-plussed.

Lord Saire was well aware that he rather fancied himself as a Royal Matchmaker. He would have liked to return to Lady Gertrude with the information that Theydon Saire would be speaking to her in the manner she desired within a few days.

But Lord Saire had not won his reputation for diplomacy without knowing how to handle the Prince.

He leaned forward to say in a voice that could not be heard by the other gentlemen at the table:

"I would like to have a chance to speak to you privately and confidentially, Sire. As a matter of fact, I need your help in several other matters which I cannot speak about at this moment."

The Prince's eyes had glinted.

He had been kept out of taking any part in political affairs for so long by his mother that he was forced to glean information from whatever source he could.

But he wished to be in the know and he was desperately frustrated at being deliberately isolated from the Foreign Office secrets.

The mere fact that Lord Saire intimated he would be told things that he could not know officially was as exciting as the offer of a drink to a thirsty man.

"I will arrange that we shall have a talk at the first opportunity, Saire," he said.

Lord Saire knew that at the moment at any rate Lady Gertrude's problems were swept from his mind.

Although he told the Prince enough to satisfy him, he was relieved that going abroad secretly and quietly without saying good-bye had doubt-less saved him from being further embroiled in *Boudoir* politics.

It was a game which all the women of the Marlborough House set played according to their own rules.

The Prince could prove a very formidable op-ponent and at times, as Lord Saire was aware, an extremely disconcerting one.

He was thankful where Gertrude was con-cerned that he did not have to risk Royal disap-proval by stating bluntly and categorically that he had no intention of ever making her his wife.

He did not think he would be deliberately os-tracised if he refused to do what the Prince wished.

Yet, stranger things had happened, and the Prince could be a very real and warm friend, but also an extremely formidable enemy.

"I have escaped!" Lord Saire said to himself.

He settled down comfortably in one of the deep arm-chairs with which his cabin was furnished and heard his valet unpacking his clothes next door.

He had brought all the newspapers with him on the train and he picked up the *Times*, read the leading article, then started on Parliamentary Reports.

It was a little time later that his valet, Cosnet, brought him the Passenger List.

"The ship's absolutely full, M'Lord," he said as he set it down on the table. "But I expects there'll be some passengers getting off at Malta and at Alexandria."

"I was afraid we might be overcrowded," Lord Saire remarked, thinking the decks would be congested when he wanted to take exercise. "Anyone we know on board, Cosnet?"

He knew his valet was as *au fait* with his friends and his many acquaintances as he was himself.

"There's that Persian gentleman, M'Lord, we met three years ago when we was staying with our Ambassador in Teheran."

"Oh, good!" Lord Saire replied. "I shall be glad to see him again!"

"There's Lord and Lady Sandford, the Honourable Mrs. Murray, and Lady Ellenton, who I think Your Lordship knows."

"Yes, of course," Lord Saire murmured.

They were all rather dull with the exception of Mrs. Murray, the wife of a diplomat, whom he had met on several occasions and thought attractive.

There was a faint smile on his lips as he returned to his newspaper.

The voyage might not be so dull after all, and Mrs. Murray with her red hair and slanting green eyes certainly bore no resemblance to Gertrude.

The dinner on the first evening in the Second Class Saloon was a surprise to Bertilla.

She had imagined that she would be able to have an individual table to herself, but she found that the passengers sat at long communal tables, decanters slung from the ceiling above their heads.

The diners sat rather close together and it had been impossible to remain reserved and uncommunicative with the persons on her right and left.

She was in fact next to a rubber planter who had been home on leave from Malaya and was eagerly looking forward to going back to his wife and three children.

He expounded at great length on the appearance of his two sons and the profits he intended to make on his plantation.

On the other side of Bertilla was an elderly Scot who was the European buyer for a Chinaman who owned several shops in Singapore.

At her end of the table the white Europeans were all placed together, but she noticed that on the other side, fortunately a long way down the room, was the Dutch-Javanese man who had stared at her when she arrived.

She was well aware that he kept looking at her all through dinner and she had the uncomfortable feeling that he intended to speak to her as soon as the meal was finished.

She circumvented him by moving away quicker than the majority of passengers and going immediately to her own cabin.

She had unpacked, and now that they were at sea the cabin did not seem so constricting or so drab.

With her own things scattered about, it seemed almost home-like.

Because they were out in the Channel and the sea was rough, Bertilla undressed and, picking up one of the books she particularly wanted to read, lay down on her bunk and turned on the reading light.

It was quite comfortable, she thought, and perhaps when she got used to the ship and the strange people aboard it she might even make a few friends.

She thought with a smile that her mother would have been horrified at her speaking to, let alone being friendly with, any of the people she had seen so far in the Second Class.

But she was well aware that even if she wished to do so, she could not mix with the First Class passengers, and she must therefore make the best of the condition in which she found herself.

The food had been edible, if not very exciting, and she was sure that if nothing else she would learn at first hand a great deal about the people who lived in the part of the world to which she was journeying.

So far she had recognised Chinese, Indians, two men who she was certain came from Bali, and of course the Dutch-Javanese.

"I think he may be rather tiresome," Bertilla told herself, and she made up her mind to make every effort to avoid him.

It was however one thing to make a decision at night and much more difficult to keep it the next day.

The sea was rough and when Bertilla went on deck wrapped in her warmest coat there were very few people to be seen.

She had intended to walk briskly round and round to take exercise, but the rolling of the ship made it impossible.

Having stayed for a little while to watch the waves breaking over the bow, she was just about to go back inside when a voice with a decidedly Dutch accent said:

"Good-morning, Miss Alvinston!"

It was the Dutch-Javanese and she replied as coldly as possible:

"Good-morning!"

"You are very brave. I thought you would not leave your cabin on such a rough day."

"I hope I am a good sailor," Bertilla replied.

She would have moved away but it was impossible to pass the man who was standing close to her without lurching into him, owing to the movement of the ship.

She therefore stood where she was, holding on to the rail, her eyes on the sea.

"I hope, Miss Alvinston, we shall be friends on this voyage."

"How do you know my name?" Bertilla enquired.

The man gave a deep laugh which seemed to come from the very depths of his somewhat stout body.

"I am not a detective," he said, "I merely asked the Purser."

Bertilla did not reply and after a moment he said:

"My name is Van da Kaempfer, and as I have said, Miss Alvinston, I hope we shall be friends. I see you are travelling alone."

"I . . . I have a lot of work to do in my cabin," Bertilla said.

It was foolish of her, she knew, but she felt as if this large man was encroaching on her, coming closer not only physically but mentally.

She had no wish to talk to him and she wanted to run away but was not quite certain how she should do so.

"Ladies who travel alone," Mr. Van da Kaempfer was saving, "need a man to look after them, to protect them. I'm offering myself in that capacity, Miss Alvinston."

"Thank you very much, but I can look after myself."

He laughed again.

"You are much too small and too pretty to do

that. Have you never thought to yourself how dangerous it is for a pretty lady such as you are to be alone in a crowd of strangers?"

There was something in his voice which made Bertilla shiver.

"It is kind of you, Mr. Van da Kaempfer, but I now wish to go back to my cabin."

"Before you do that," he said, "let me buy you a drink. We will go to the Cocktail Bar. I am sure you would find that a glass of champagne would make it easier for you to find your 'sea legs.'"

"Thank you, no," Bertilla replied.

She turned round as she spoke but the ship gave a sudden roll and threw her against Mr. Van da Kaempfer.

He laughed and put his arm through hers.

"Let me help you," he said. "As I have already said, there are many dangers at sea and the waves constitute one of them."

Without making a scene it was impossible for Bertilla to extricate herself from his arm.

He drew her firmly along the deck and through a heavy door which took them inside to the heat and warmth and away from the wind which had whipped Bertilla's fair hair round her cheeks.

"Now for that nice glass of champagne," Mr. Van da Kaempfer said, leading Bertilla towards the Cocktail Lounge.

"No, thank you. I do not drink," she replied.

"Then it is time you began," he answered.

With an effort that was almost a struggle Bertilla pulled her arm from Mr. Van da

Kaempfer's and before he could prevent her she hurried away from him.

She thought as she went that she heard him laugh and she was conscious when she reached her cabin that her heart was beating quickly and her lips felt dry.

"I am being stupid . . . very stupid," she admonished herself.

After all, what was there to be afraid of?

The man was common and pushing, but it was to be expected that he would think since she was travelling alone that she would be only too pleased to accept his hospitality.

'I shall simply ignore him,' she thought.

At the same time, she had the uncomfortable feeling that it might be a very difficult thing to do.

Chapter Three

"I must go back to my own cabin."

Rosemary Murray spoke softly and with infinite regret in her voice.

"That would be sensible," Lord Saire agreed.

She stretched her arms out in a despairing gesture.

"God, how I hate being sensible. It is what I have to be all my life!"

She turned round to put her head on his bare shoulder as she said passionately:

"But I am not complaining. An interlude like this makes up for everything, even for the utter boredom that I shall find in Egypt."

Lord Saire did not answer and after a moment she went on:

"If only I could come with you to Singapore and did not have to get off at Alexandria."

Her voice vibrated and with a little throb in it she said:

"Promise that you will not forget me. I shall be praying that we shall meet again someday, somewhere, and that everything will be as wonderful as it is now."

"I shall be hoping that, too," Lord Saire said.

But he knew as he spoke that he was being insincere.

He had enjoyed this flirtation, if that was the right word for it, with Mrs. Murray, between the White Cliffs of Dover and Alexandria.

Her red hair had been a promise of everything he expected: that she was fiery, tempestuous, and as passionate in her own way as Lady Gertrude had been.

But inevitably he had had enough, and he knew that when she went ashore at Alexandria tomorrow there would be no regrets on his side but rather a feeling of relief.

As she put on the diaphanous negligee in which she had crept along the passage to his cabin, Lord Saire watched her speculatively and wondered why she was the type of woman of whom one tired so quickly.

There was no doubt that she was beautiful, her figure was exquisite, and she enjoyed love-making with a primitive greediness that had an attraction all its own.

And yet his first ardour had been replaced by a boredom that had grown day by day as they steamed across the Mediterranean, until now he was actually looking forward to tomorrow.

He put on a long brocade robe and as he stood looking at her, Rosemary Murray turned towards him with a sound that was almost a sob.

"I love you! Oh, Theydon, I love you!" she cried. "You have captured my heart. I shall never find another man who could take your place."

She flung her arms round his neck and her lips were lifted to his and he kissed her as he was expected to do.

"You must go," he said quietly as her body moved against his. "You know in a ship, more than anywhere else, the walls have ears."

Rosemary Murray gave a deep sigh.

"I love you! I shall love you for all eternity," she said dramatically, "and we shall meet again — yes, Theydon, we shall meet again — I know that!"

Lord Saire opened the door, looked out to see if the passageway was clear, then beckoned to Rosemary Murray to leave.

She did so, kissing his cheek as she passed him, the exotic fragrance of her perfume seeming to encompass him and leave behind a lingering fragrance on the air as she moved swiftly and silently away.

Lord Saire shut the door of his cabin and gave a deep sigh.

It was over!

This was the finish of another *affaire de coeur* which had ended in exactly the same way as all his others had.

He thought that D'Arcy Charington would laugh if he knew what he was feeling, and would undoubtedly ask:

"What are you expecting, Theydon? What are you looking for?"

The trouble was, he did not know the answer.

He saw that left behind on the chair in his cabin was a photograph.

Rosemary Murray had brought it with her when she had crept into his cabin two hours earlier.

"I knew you would want it to remember me by," she had said.

He saw that she had signed it: "Yours until eternity, Rosemary."

It was indiscreet and the sort of thing that no sensible married woman would do.

But another inevitability of his love-affairs was that women trusted Lord Saire not only with their photographs but also with innumerable passionate and wildly indiscreet letters such as would be utterly damning to say the very least of it should they ever be read by an outsider.

Yet women gave Lord Saire not only their hearts and their bodies, but also their good names.

In consequence he was always extremely careful, where it was possible, not to make them suffer for their own indiscretions.

It was he rather than they who took care to protect them from unnecessary gossip.

It was he who persuaded them not to come boldly to his house in London as they invariably wished to do, or to make it very obvious to all and sundry when they met in public that they were in love with him.

"Damn it all, they seem to want to commit Social suicide!" he said once to D'Arcy Charington.

His friend had laughed.

"They do not care how heavy the chain that binds them," he replied, "as long as it binds you too."

But somehow, mainly because he was extremely intelligent, Lord Saire had managed so far to avoid an open scandal.

That was not to say that he was not talked about, and people suspected a great deal of what had actually happened.

But that was a very different thing from proving it.

Lord Saire made very certain that jealous husbands and the world in general found it difficult to produce concrete evidence of any indiscretion.

He looked at the clock by his bed and saw that it was nearly two o'clock.

He was just about to get back into bed when he felt a sudden distaste for Rosemary Murray's scent, which lingered on the pillows, and was annoyed at the fact that the bed itself looked untidy and the sheets were crumpled.

On an impulse he pulled off his long robe and dressed himself with a quickness that would have annoyed his valet, who thought himself indispensable.

He took an overcoat from the wardrobe and hatless walked out of his cabin and onto the covered deck.

Although it was so late there were still sounds of loud laughter coming from the Smoking-Room.

There the habitual hard-drinking passengers would still be sitting on the plush-covered sofas with their drinks on tables in front of them.

There were some people who seemed never to go to sleep on board ship, but the Saloon was empty and there were only a few tired stewards moving round to notice Lord Saire walking briskly along the covered deck.

He felt in need of air and climbed higher onto the top deck where games would be arranged as soon as the ship was in calmer waters.

In the daytime the place was usually noisy, filled with men taking exercise in one way or another, or children playing Hide-and-Seek round the funnels, masts, and superstructure.

Part of the canvas awning which would cover the deck as soon as they got into the brilliant sunshine of the Red Sea was already being erected.

But three quarters of it was still open to the night and Lord Saire looked up at the stars and felt the air cool on his face.

It had been very rough in the Bay of Biscay, but ever since they had reached the Mediterranean the weather had mellowed and been exceptionally warm for the time of year.

It grew cool at night, however.

But the nearer they had sailed to Alexandria the warmer it had become, and Lord Saire looked forward as few other people did to the heat of the Red Sea.

The sun, he told himself, would burn away the

memories of the thick fogs and sharp frosts of England.

The deck was completely deserted and he sauntered along with his hands in his pockets, thinking not of Rosemary Murray, as might have been expected, but of his mission to the East and the different people he would be meeting there.

It still gave him a sense of adventure to journey to places that he had never been to before.

He knew that on this trip he would visit new lands and he was determined to learn a great deal about their history and customs before he arrived.

He had walked in a semi-circle and was approaching the stern when out of the shadows beside one of the funnels he heard a woman's voice say:

"Lord . . . Saire!"

He turned his head in annoyance, impatient at having his thoughts interrupted, and he saw someone small approach him.

In the light of the stars there was a very pale face with huge eyes lifted to his.

"Forgive me . . . please forgive me . . . but I . . . need your help," a voice said.

Suddenly he remembered where he had heard it before and where he had seen that heart-shaped face.

"Miss Alvinston!" he exclaimed. "I had no idea you were on board."

"I should not be up here, but I was . . . h-hiding, and actually I was wondering how I could . . . approach you . . . to ask you for h-help."

"You are hiding?" Lord Saire repeated. "But from whom?"

Bertilla glanced nervously over her shoulder as if she felt someone might be listening.

As she did so she put out her hand to hold on to the rail of the ship and Lord Saire saw that she was trembling.

"What has upset you?" he asked. "And why are you here at this hour of the night?"

"Th-that is what I . . . wanted to tell you," she answered, "and I know . . . I am being a nuisance and I should not . . . bother you, but I do not know what . . . else I can . . . do."

There was something so pathetic and so frightened in the way she spoke that Lord Saire said:

"You know I will help you if it is at all possible. Shall we sit down somewhere?"

He looked round as he spoke and realised that the deck-chairs had all been cleared away for the night, but there was a fixed wooden seat beneath one of the masts.

"We will sit there," he said, and put his hand under her elbow to take her towards it.

They walked a few feet to the seat and sat down.

As Bertilla turned herself sideways towards him she pushed a chiffon scarf back from her hair and he saw how fair it was in the starlight.

She clasped her hands together and said:

"You will think it very . . . foolish and very . . .

stupid of me, but I do not . . . know what to . . . do and there is . . . no-one else I can ask."

"Suppose you start at the beginning," Lord Saire suggested, "and tell me why you are here. I thought you were in London, riding in the Park."

"I . . . know," Bertilla said, "but Mama had . . . arranged to send me . . . away."

"Where to?"

"To Sarawak . . . to my aunt who is a . . . Missionary there."

"A Missionary?" Lord Saire exclaimed.

Bertilla nodded.

"Y-yes. Mama thinks I should be a M-Missionary too, and there was . . . nowhere else I could go."

Bertilla's voice revealed far more than she said of how the idea had not only frightened but horrified her.

Lord Saire's lips tightened, remembering that he had always disliked Lady Alvinston and thought her a hard, unfeeling woman, and now he was certain that his instinct about her had been right.

"So you are going to Sarawak," he said aloud. "And who is travelling with you?"

"N-no-one," Bertilla answered, "and that is the . . . trouble."

"No-one?"

Lord Saire could hardly believe what he heard.

That any woman as a Leader of Society should send her daughter, especially one so young and inexperienced as Bertilla, half-way round the world without a Chaperon was so incredible that he could hardly believe it to be the truth.

He was well aware that girls often travelled to India and other parts of the Empire to join their parents or friends.

But some sort of Chaperon was always arranged for the sea-voyage, and often the wives of Senior Army Officers or diplomats would find themselves responsible for half a dozen protégés who at times were a considerable nuisance.

But to send a girl alone with no-one to look after her was so incredible that Lord Saire found himself for the moment speechless.

"I realise that I am old enough to look after myself," Bertilla was saying, "but you see . . . I am travelling . . . S-Second Class, and . . . and there is . . . a man . . ."

"What man?" Lord Saire enquired almost sharply.

"He . . . he is D-Dutch," Bertilla said, "although I think he has some . . . Javanese blood in him, and he will not . . . l-leave me alone."

Lord Saire said nothing and she gave a little cry as she went on, with her hands clasped together:

"You will think I am an . . . idiot . . . as Mama always says I am . . . but I cannot avoid him . . . I spend nearly all my time in my . . . cabin . . . but . . ."

Her voice died away but she was obviously feeling for words and Lord Saire said quietly:

"What has happened?"

He knew instinctively without Bertilla telling him that things had reached a climax.

"The last few nights . . . since we have been in the . . . Mediterranean, a . . . s-steward has brought me . . . presents," Bertilla replied, "chocolates and other things that you can . . . buy on board . . . I send them back . . . but he keeps writing me n-notes and requests that I should . . . join him for a drink."

She gave a little sigh.

"He . . . t-tried to make me do that . . . the first night on board . . . but I ran away . . . I have tried to keep running . . . but it does not . . . s-seem to h-help."

"What happened tonight?" Lord Saire asked quietly.

"When I . . . went to my . . . cabin after d-dinner . . . I always hurry out of the D-Dining-Room in case he should . . . follow me . . . I shut my c-cabin door."

She paused and Lord Saire could see the fear in her eyes as she said almost in a whisper:

"The k-key had gone and so had . . . the b-bolt!"

Lord Saire stiffened, then he said angrily:

"This is disgraceful! It should not occur on any decent ship!"

He guessed exactly what had happened: the steward had been heavily bribed and the supervision on the Second Class deck was nothing like so strict as that on the First Class.

"So you came up here," he said after a moment.

"I . . . did not know what . . . else to d-do," Bertilla said. "As you know . . . I am not . . . supposed to leave the Second Class deck, but then . . . he would have . . . l-looked for me and I would have been unable to . . . escape."

The terror in her voice was very obvious, and Lord Saire realised that this man — and he could visualise exactly what sort of creature he was — had terrorised the child.

She was obviously frantic at the idea that she might not be able to go on avoiding him.

It was impossible, Lord Saire thought, to blame the man too much.

To him a woman travelling alone would be fair game, and doubtless as a Dutchman it had never crossed his mind that Bertilla might have any Social status, since she was unaccompanied by a Chaperon or even by a lady's-maid.

Lord Saire realised that Bertilla was looking at him with an expression in her eyes that reminded him of a spaniel he once had owned which used to look at him in very much the same way with a wholehearted trust.

"You are not to worry yourself," he said.

As he spoke he put out his hand and laid it on Bertilla's as they were clenched together in her lap.

As he touched them he gave a little start.

"You are frozen!" he exclaimed. "But of course — if you have been sitting here for some hours you must be very cold."

"I . . . came away in such a . . . hurry," Bertilla explained, "that I . . . snatched the first coat I could find. I am afraid it is a very . . . thin one."

"I am going to take you below," Lord Saire said, "and give you a warm drink. Then I will sort out your problem, that I promise you."

"I am . . . so sorry to . . . worry you."

"It is no worry," he answered, "and you did quite right in coming to me for assistance. I only wish you had done so sooner."

Bertilla drew in her breath.

"You are so kind . . . but Mama would be very . . . angry if she knew I was . . . speaking to you."

Lord Saire remembered the lies, and he had known they were lies, that Lady Alvinston had told him about Bertilla.

She might look very young, he thought, but no one as experienced as he was where women were concerned would believe her to be fourteen.

Also, he very much doubted if she would ever have done anything so drastic as to merit being expelled from school.

"I suggest," he said with a smile, "that we forget your mother. One thing which is reassuring is that she will not know what we are doing at this moment."

He saw Bertilla smile.

"I am sure it is wrong to think like that . . . but, as you say . . . Mama will not know."

"Then come with me," Lord Saire said.

They went down the companionway to the next deck and as he opened the door Bertilla felt the warmth come out to her, a warmth that seemed to envelop her protectively.

She had felt very cold on deck and she had known that at first it was not only the chill air of the night but also that she was so frightened.

It was impossible to tell Lord Saire how every day seemed to bring a new fear from the closer encroachment of Mr. Van da Kaempfer.

Wherever she went he seemed to be waiting for her.

She found it hard to eat because his eyes were on her. She dreaded a knock on her cabin door which told her there was another present or note from him.

She wondered desperately whether it would be wise to confront him and tell him to leave her alone and threaten that if he did not do so she would speak to the Captain.

Then she thought it would be impossible to say such things to him in public, while if they were alone . . . she felt herself shiver at what he might do if there was no-one else there to prevent him.

She had never actively been afraid of a man in her life before.

She had of course met men, usually rather old and dull ones, in Bath with her Aunt Margaret.

They talked to her in the Pump-Room where they were drinking the waters, and there had been various retired Army Officers and their wives whom Aunt Margaret entertained to tea or occasionally to dinner.

Although they had paid her compliments and often teased her in a pleasant and informal manner, there had certainly been nothing frightening about them.

Nothing that had made her shrink with her whole mind and body as she did when faced with Mr. Van da Kaempfer.

Bertilla was very innocent and she had no idea what a love-affair between a man and a woman actually entailed.

She knew it meant more than an exchange of kisses, and that a far greater intimacy was enjoyed by those who were paired together in the house-parties which her mother attended at great mansions all over the country.

She had once heard her father and mother having a row over a man who, her father had alleged in a voice of fury, had been taking liberties which he would never condone with the woman who bore his name.

"You are ridiculous, George!" Lady Alvinston said scornfully. "If Francis loves me to distraction, what can I do about it?"

"You need not encourage the fellow, for one thing," Sir George had thundered, "and if you think I will let you go alone to Dovacourt next week with that young whippersnapper doubtless sleeping in the next room, you are much mistaken!"

"Really, George! Your insinuations are intolerable!" Lady Alvinston said, but not very convincingly.

Bertilla had found it very confusing, but she had wondered if Francis, whoever he might be, was her mother's lover.

She had read about lovers in her history-books, and although they did not dwell on such things at school, it was impossible to ignore the existence of ladies who decorated the Court of Charles II.

The position of Madame de Maintenon and Madame de Pompadour in France was not concealed, nor was the behaviour of George IV not only with Mrs. Fitzherbert but also in his old age with Lady Hereford and Lady Coningham.

However skillfully such relationships were glossed over in the Class-Room, as Bertilla read extensively she became aware that love was a very strong weapon in any woman's hands, and as a weapon women had undoubtedly used it all down the ages.

But love, she was quite certain, was something very different from what Mr. Van da Kaempfer wanted.

She knew that whatever it was she would die rather than allow him to touch her, and even to think of his thick lips made her feel physically sick.

Lord Saire was leading her not into the Saloon, although it was deserted, but into the Writing-Room, which he guessed would be completely empty at this time of the night.

There were several tables with blotters and sunken ink-bottles on them, and there was also at one end a comfortable sofa.

"Sit down," he said to Bertilla, "I am going to fetch you something hot to drink which will prevent you from catching cold."

In the light which glittered on her fair hair he could see her eyes raised to his with the expression in them which had struck him so forcibly when they were on deck.

He smiled beguilingly and added:

"You will be quite safe if I leave you here for two or three minutes. I am only going to find a steward."

He went away, but he was in fact longer than two or three minutes, and before he returned a steward came into the room with a tray.

It contained a pot of coffee, one cup, and two glasses of brandy.

"Milk, Madam?" he enquired as he poured out the coffee.

There was something in his calm, ordinary voice which made Bertilla feel her fears and agitation beginning to subside.

She had been terrified not only by Mr. Van da Kaempfer but also of speaking to Lord Saire.

Her mother would be furious, she knew that, and unless she had been desperate, knowing how outrageous Lady Alvinston would think it would be, she would never have dared to approach him.

He came back and as he neared the sofa on which she was sitting he took off his overcoat and threw it down on a chair.

"Feeling warmer?" he asked.

She looked up at him and he saw there was a faint flush on her pale cheeks.

"The coffee tastes wonderful!" she answered.

"I want you to drink a glass of brandy."

She wrinkled her nose.

"I do not like brandy."

"That is not important," he replied. "The brandy is medicinal. The nights in the Mediterranean can be very treacherous, and I know you will not wish to stay in bed for the next three or four days."

He saw in the darkness of her eyes what she feared and he said quickly:

"Do not worry. I have spoken to the Purser and your things are being moved at this very moment from your cabin up into the First Class."

Bertilla looked at him in astonishment, then she said:

"I am . . . afraid I cannot . . . pay the difference."

"There will be nothing to pay," Lord Saire answered quietly. "I explained to the Purser the uncomfortable circumstances in which you have found yourself. He was deeply apologetic. As someone left the ship at Malta a cabin is available and it has been allotted to you without your incurring any further charge."

"Are you sure of that?" Bertilla asked.

"I told you to trust me," Lord Saire replied.

"Oh . . . thank you! Thank you more than I can

say! I might have guessed . . . I felt certain you would . . . save me."

"Then make sure of it and drink up your brandy!"

She obeyed him, only making a little grimace as the liquid seemed to seer her throat.

"I will drink some more coffee to take away the taste," she said.

"That is a sensible idea," he agreed, "and now I want you to forget this unfortunate experience and enjoy the rest of your voyage."

"He will not be . . . able to approach me . . . now that I am on a . . . different deck," Bertilla said in a low voice.

She made the statement as if to reassure herself.

"You will not be troubled any more by the man in question," Lord Saire said sharply. "At the same time, as I am sure you must be aware, you should not be travelling alone."

"Mama could not afford to send anyone with me."

"I cannot help thinking it would be better if she had not sent you to Sarawak anyway," Lord Saire said. "It is a very primitive, underdeveloped country, although, as I expect you know, the Rajah is a white man."

"I have heard of Sir Charles Brooke, but otherwise I know very little about it."

She looked round as she spoke and saw that the Library which was so eulogised in the brochure issued by the P. & O. was actually situated in the Writing-Room.

One whole wall was covered with books, locked away behind glass doors.

Lord Saire followed the direction of her eyes.

"I think you will find quite a lot here that will interest you," he said. "And if not, I will try to buy you a book about Sarawak when we reach Alexandria tomorrow."

"You are so kind . . . so very, very kind," Bertilla said. "I was looking forward to seeing Alexandria, but perhaps it would be unwise for me to go ashore."

She was thinking of Mr. Van da Kaempfer, and Lord Saire said:

"You certainly cannot walk about Alexandria alone. I will try to make arrangements for someone to take you if I cannot do so myself."

Bertilla shook her head.

"I have no wish to bother you," she said. "Please forget about me. Now that I am on this deck, I am sure I can look after myself."

"I am afraid I have little confidence in that," he said with a smile which took the edge off his words. "I have a feeling that you are somewhat accident-prone."

She looked at him apprehensively and he went on:

"Porters run you down with luggage; you find ogres where they are least expected; and goodness knows what will happen to you in the Red Sea or when you get among the head-hunters in Sarawak!"

Lord Saire was only being amusing and speaking as he would have spoken to any woman of his acquaintance, but as he saw the fear leap into Bertilla's eyes he added quickly:

"I am only teasing you. I am quite certain that your bad luck, if that is what it is, has already blown itself out like a north wind."

"It was good luck for me . . . that you were here," Bertilla said. "When I saw you come aboard it was somehow comforting to know there was another person in the whole ship whom I knew and who had been kind to me. But I did not wish to . . . encroach on you."

There were few women in his life, Lord Saire thought, who had said that to him. They were always too ready to encroach, to force themselves upon him whether he wished it or not.

"You are not encroaching and you are not being a nuisance, and I promise you it is no bother to do what I can for you," he answered. "There is a journey ahead which I hope you will enjoy. Personally, I love the heat and I find it an adventure to see new countries and meet the people who belong to them."

"I have been thinking that too," Bertilla said. "But it is only that I am so . . . stupid and get . . . frightened quite unnecessarily."

"In this case it has been far from unnecessary," Lord Saire answered. "It was something you could not help, so do not blame yourself. Just forget it ever happened and look forward to tomorrow."

He spoke kindly as he might have done to a child, and as Bertilla looked up at him he saw that there were tears in her grey eyes.

"No-one has ever been so . . . kind to me . . . before," she said with a catch in her breath, "and I know that if Papa were . . . alive he would want to thank you. You must . . . believe me when I say . . . thank you from the very . . . bottom of my heart."

Having seen Bertilla to her new cabin, Lord Saire returned to his own.

As he got into bed, he was not only feeling sorry for the child but disgusted by her mother's behaviour.

It might have been what he expected, he thought, of the much-acclaimed beauties who, as he had told D'Arcy, looked like goddesses on Olympus but obviously behaved like devils in their own homes.

Bertilla had, however, set him a problem that required a lot of his intelligence to solve.

He was well aware that if he constituted himself her Guardian during the next stage of the journey, it would cause an enormous amount of comment.

He was quite certain that the gossips were already chattering like a lot of parrots about his interest in Mrs. Murray.

However careful they had been, they could not have prevented the other passengers being aware that they walked round the deck together, had their chairs side by side, and that Mrs. Murray's green eyes when she looked at him were very revealing.

Although it might be difficult for people to prove an even closer relationship, they would certainly speculate as to how far the affair had gone.

To appear immediately with Bertilla, young though she was, would be, Lord Saire knew, to make her the talking point of the women who had nothing else to interest them as the ship moved down the Suez Canal.

At the same time, he could not leave Bertilla alone with no-one to talk to and perhaps still apprehensive that the Dutchman might in some way make contact with her.

Lord Saire had known women in almost every mood — passionate, angry, fiery with desire, or vitriolic with recrimination — but he could not remember ever before having coped with a woman who was afraid.

He had thought that Bertilla trembling, her lips quivering and her fingers locked together, was very pathetic.

He thought too that he had never known a woman whose eyes were so expressive that they actually mirrored the emotion pulsating inside her.

"Millicent Alvinston ought to be shot!" he told himself aloud in the darkness.

He decided that if it was the last thing he did he would somehow see that Bertilla was properly looked after.

What would happen when the voyage ended was something out of his control, but he was well aware of the depression in her tone when she told him she was to be a Missionary.

He had some idea of what her aunt was like, having come in contact with a great number of Missionaries in one way or another.

Although the majority of them were dedicated men who really believed they had a vocation to save the souls of the heathen, the women were usually frustrated, hard-hearted, and often aggressive.

They had been forced into the life because there was no alternative but to follow their husbands to foreign lands when they would much rather have stayed at home.

'Poor girl, what a future!' Lord Saire thought.

He knew that trying to convert the heathen from that faith of their fathers was a thankless task.

Before he fell asleep, however, he came to one decision about Bertilla.

The next morning after Lord Saire had taken his usual exercise round the deck before most people were awake, he sought out Lady Sandford.

He had known her for some years but because she was a boring woman he had done his best so far to avoid her during the voyage.

Now he sat himself down beside her deck-chair and, having asked after the health of her husband, said in a tone he knew most women found impossible to resist:

"I need your advice."

Lady Sandford looked startled but gratified.

Her husband had spoken warmly of Lord Saire's achievements, but she thought he was rather a stuck-up young man and had realised as soon as the ship left harbour that he had no intention of burdening himself with their company.

But now she put down the knitting on which she was habitually engaged and said with an ingenuous note in her voice:

"My advice, Lord Saire?"

"I have just discovered that Lady Alvinston's daughter is on board," Lord Saire answered, "and to tell the truth it has put me in rather an embarrassing position."

Lady Sandford was listening attentively and he went on:

"As it happens, I saw Lady Alvinston at Marlborough House the night before I left, and she told me her daughter was travelling out to Sarawak. However, it slipped my mind."

He saw a flicker in Lady Sandford's small, unattractive eyes, and knew that she was aware of the reason why everything had slipped his mind except a certain red-haired, green-eyed passenger.

"I learnt yesterday that owing to a mistake by the Steamship Line, and a very reprehensible one, I may add," Lord Saire went on, "Miss

Alvinston had been put on the Second Class deck."

"The Second Class!" Lady Sandford exclaimed.

"It was an oversight or a clerk's error," Lord Saire said airily, "but as you can imagine, I feel very guilty that I had not made enquiries before as to her whereabouts."

"It really is a disgraceful mistake and quite un-forgivable," Lady Sandford replied. "What has happened now?"

"I understand the Purser has moved her onto this deck," Lord Saire said. "Naturally the girl has had no-one to speak to below, and I should imagine that she is feeling rather disturbed by having to endure such an experience."

"Of course there may be some decent people in the Second Class," Lady Sandford said doubt-fully, "but I am afraid there are a great many — *foreigners*."

The way she spoke the word made it quite un-necessary to add what she thought of such undesirable aliens, and Lord Saire said quickly:

"That is why, Lady Sandford, I am in such a dilemma to know what to do so late in the day."

Lady Sandford smiled.

"I suppose, Lord Saire, you are asking me to take charge of this young woman?"

"It would be just like your usual warm-hearted generosity," Lord Saire said in all sincerity.

Then he added with an almost impish note in his voice:

"I promise you, Lady Sandford, I am quite at

96

a loss as to how to behave when it comes to young girls. It is a very long time since my 'débutante days.' "

Lady Sandford laughed.

"Leave it to me, Lord Saire. What is this girl's name?"

Lord Saire put his hand up to his forehead.

"Now — let me think — Lady Alvinston told me what it was, but I am afraid I was not listening very intently. It begins with a 'B' — yes, that is right — Belinda — or Bertilda — something like that."

"Do not give it another thought," Lady Sandford said with a smile.

"You are kindness itself!" Lord Saire exclaimed. "And I shall always be grateful to you for covering up my shortcomings!"

"I quite understand you had other things to think about," Lady Sandford said with a touch of irony. "Indeed I think, at this moment, there is someone trying to attract your attention."

Lord Saire looked round and saw that Mrs. Murray had come onto the deck.

She was looking very alluring in a gown of green silk that matched her eyes and a large straw hat which shaded her face and her red hair.

"I think Mrs. Murray wishes to say good-bye to me," he said.

"I am sure she does," Lady Sandford replied.

Lord Saire left her side to go blithely towards two green eyes which were looking at him reproachfully.

Bertilla was astonished and at the same time glad of Lady Sandford's almost gushing approach when she went out on deck as the ship docked in Alexandria Harbour.

"I have been looking for you, Miss Alvinston," Lady Sandford said, "as I have only just learnt that you are on board. I know your mother, my dear, and I am sure she would like me to look after you during the long hot days that lie ahead of us when we reach the Red Sea."

"That is very kind of you," Bertilla said, rather surprised.

"You must have a deck-chair next to me," Lady Sandford said, "and I will arrange for you to sit next to my husband and me at meals. Of course, we are at the Captain's Table, but now that Mrs. Murray has left there will be an empty place."

"Thank you very much," Bertilla replied.

She did in fact find Lady Sandford very kind when later in the day she took her ashore and they drove in a carriage through the streets of Alexandria so that Bertilla could see the famous waterfront and some of the ancient ruins.

There were several things that Bertilla would have liked to buy, but she told herself she must conserve what little money she had in case she had expenses later on in the journey, especially when she had to change ships at Singapore.

She had learnt, somewhat to her consternation, that when she arrived there the steamer only left every two weeks.

She would have to find a very cheap Hotel, because it would be disastrous if she ran out of money before she could proceed on her journey to join her aunt.

She tried not to think too much about what would happen once she reached Sarawak, but she knew it was like a dark cloud on the horizon every day that she drew nearer and nearer to Aunt Agatha.

Even to say the name was to conjure up the fears her aunt had instilled in her as a child and memories of her harsh voice which had always seemed discordant when she was speaking to her father.

She had made no bones about the fact that she disliked children, unless they had to be converted to Christianity.

That evening when she was having coffee beside Lady Sandford in the Saloon, he came walking across the room towards them.

She thought he looked very smart and there was no other man in the whole ship to compare with him.

"Good-evening, Lady Sandford," he said. "Good-evening, Miss Alvinston."

"Good . . . evening!"

Bertilla wondered why it was difficult to say such an ordinary word and somehow she sounded almost as if she were stammering.

"Bertilla and I had a most interesting time in Alexandria," Lady Sandford said. "We enjoyed it, did we not, dear?"

"It was wonderful!" Bertilla said. "I had no idea that the town was so beautiful."

"I am sure you will find some books in the Library which will tell you of the history of it," Lord Saire said.

He spoke, Bertilla thought, indifferently, as if the subject did not interest him.

Then he said in a meaningful manner to Lady Sandford:

"I just came to say thank you. I have a lot of work to do which I am afraid has been rather neglected so far on the voyage, so you must excuse me if I go to my cabin and settle down to my papers."

Lady Sandford smiled.

"You do not have to thank me, Lord Saire," she said. "It is a very great pleasure to have Bertilla with me. George is always like a bear with a sore head when he is at sea, and I find it delightful to have someone young to talk to."

Lord Saire bade them good-night, and as he walked away Bertilla watched him go a little wistfully.

He had no sooner disappeared through the door of the Saloon than Lady Ellenton, whom Bertilla had already met with Lady Sandford, came and sat down beside them.

She was about thirty-five, the wife of a Colonial Administrator, and very fair and fluffy. Young men out from England for the first time found her irresistible.

"He is fascinating, is he not?" she asked Lady Sandford.

"Lord Saire?" Lady Sandford enquired. "I believe a great number of people find him so."

"It is not surprising so many women, of course including Lady Gertrude Lindley, lose their hearts over him!"

"I have never met Lady Gertrude," Lady Sandford said firmly.

"But you knew Daisy?"

"Yes, of course!"

"Well, she has hardly recovered, even now. Oh, dear, the trouble handsome men cause in our lives!"

Lady Ellenton spoke complacently, then said with a little laugh:

"You know his new nick-name, I suppose?"

"I have no idea," Lady Sandford replied, busy with her knitting. At the same time, Bertilla was aware that she was listening.

Lady Ellenton bent a little nearer so that it was hard for Bertilla to hear what she said, and yet she did hear it.

"'The Love Pirate'!" Lady Ellenton said. "That is what they call him, and very appropriately I think."

"Do you? But why?" Lady Sandford asked.

"Because he plunders every woman he fancies, and having taken all their treasure goes off in search for more! That is exactly what a pirate does!"

Lady Ellenton giggled, but Bertilla thought

that there was something spiteful behind her eyes and in her voice.

'She is jealous!' she thought. 'She would like Lord Saire to look at her, but she is not nearly attractive enough!'

Chapter Four

Someone came to stand beside Bertilla at the ship's rail and she knew without turning her head who it was.

They had reached the Malacca Straits after the long voyage through the Red Sea, then rounding Ceylon and through the Andaman Sea.

Now the Malay Peninsula was on the left and it seemed to Bertilla to be more beautiful than she could possibly have expected it to be.

They were steaming fairly close along the shore and there were the great forests of trees which she had learnt from her guide-book included species of the bread fruit, mangosteen, nutmeg, and mango, besides oaks with evergreen leaves.

She was trying to identify them when Lord Saire asked:

"What are you looking for?"

She turned her face to him with a smile to reply:

"Please tell me everything about this magical,

beautiful country. I am so afraid of missing something."

He laughed before he answered:

"You set me an impossible task. There is so much both old and new in Malaya that every time I come back I feel I ought to write a history-book about it."

"I have been reading about Sir Thomas Stamford Raffles, who founded Singapore," Bertilla said, "and I feel you could be like him."

Lord Saire looked surprised, then leaning over the rail beside her he asked:

"Would you like to explain what you mean by that?"

"I feel that you could build up a great port or create a country as he did by sheer personality and determination."

"You think that is what I have?"

There was a mocking note in Lord Saire's voice but Bertilla replied quite seriously:

"I am sure you have, and the world needs men like you."

She spoke gravely and in a way impersonally.

Looking at her profile as she stared at the trees, the primitive houses built on stilts, and the children splashing at the water's edge, Lord Saire thought she was unlike any woman he had ever met before in his life.

In his anxiety not to compromise her in any way he had not singled her out or talked privately with her until Alexandria was far behind them and they were halfway down the Red Sea.

Then he had learnt that she had a habit of slipping away from the crowds just as he himself always liked to do.

He would find her hidden in some isolated part of the deck where few other people went, and she rose very early in the morning when there were only health enthusiasts about, intent on taking exercise.

It was then that he talked to her and found her extremely intelligent and at the same time mentally very humble.

The few women of his acquaintance who had brains were so keen on showing them off and parading them that they became almost intolerable in the superiority they claimed over what they considered "the mere male."

Bertilla would ask him questions, her grey eyes wide and serious as she listened to what he had to tell her.

And he knew that she stored what she learnt in her mind, adding to the knowledge she had already accumulated from the books in the Library and those he had bought for her in Alexandria.

He had had the latter sent to her cabin so that no-one should know that he had made her a present of them, and Bertilla had been wise enough not to thank him publicly.

But he received a little note written in a neat, upright hand-writing, most unlike the scrawling flowery lettering typical of the correspondence he usually received from women.

Bertilla was, he noticed now, very plainly dressed as she had been all through the voyage.

But her gown of cheap muslin became her in a manner he could not explain, but which he thought must be attributed to a natural elegance which would make anything she wore seem attractive.

"I wonder," he asked aloud, "whether I would be happy living permanently in this part of the world, even if I had the position and authority of Sir Stamford Raffles."

"You might become a White Rajah like Sir Charles Brooke," Bertilla suggested.

Lord Saire was aware that her mind was permanently on the place to which she was journeying and which would be her home perhaps for the rest of her life.

He had told her about the romance of Sarawak and that, because its Ruler was a White Rajah, Sir Charles Brooke, it had a unique place in history.

He told Bertilla, far more excitingly than any book could have done, how the first White Rajah, James Brooke, in reward for his services in helping to crush a rebellion had been nominated Rajah of Sarawak in 1841 by the Sultan of Borneo, and now his nephew had succeeded him.

"The people are a very happy and very pleasant race," he told Bertilla.

"But . . . they are head-hunters!"

"I think the White Rajahs have done a great deal to suppress that very deplorable custom," he said with a smile, "but the Dyaks are gentle, honest, and touchingly kind. Their women too are beautiful and completely fearless."

"Is head-hunting their religion?" Bertilla asked.

"They worship no gods except a long-dead hero, and they have no priests and no religious ceremonies."

"Then why, if they are so happy . . . ?"

She stopped speaking, but Lord Saire knew what she had been about to say.

"Wherever the British establish their rule, the Missionaries follow," he explained. "They believe they are appointed by God to convert people of other nationalities into Christians whether they like it or not."

There was a cynical note in his voice which told Bertilla he did not believe in such proselytizing, and after a moment she said:

"Do you believe that someone who is not a Christian cannot go to Heaven?"

"Good Lord, no!" Lord Saire replied. "Besides, if there is such a place as Heaven, I am quite certain there is a large number of different ones."

She smiled as he went on:

"A Heaven for the Christians, Nirvana for the Buddhists, and a very alluring Paradise filled with beautiful women for the Mohammedans! I am sure too the Dyaks have a special place where they can collect any number of heads without hurting anyone!"

Bertilla laughed.

"That is exactly what I want to believe. But I am sure religion is a private thing and very personal, and therefore if people are happy it is wrong to interfere."

He felt that, although she was saying this to him, she would find it difficult to say the same thing to her aunt when she reached Sarawak; and because it was impossible for him not to know how much she dreaded the end of her journey he said kindly:

"Forget the future and enjoy today."

"That is what I have been doing all the time on this fascinating voyage," Bertilla said. "At night when there is phosphorus on the waves I feel as if the ship is enchanted and we shall go on sailing in her forever and ever, never to come to port."

"It is a nice idea in theory," Lord Saire smiled, "but can you imagine how bored we should all become with each other? And how bitterly a large number of the people would be quarrelling on their second time round the world."

Bertilla laughed.

"That is true," she agreed. "Lady Ellenton and Lady Sandford both became so irritable at the whist-table last night that they are not speaking this morning."

"The only way that your enchanted ship could be a happy one," Lord Saire said, "is if there was no-one aboard but yourself and perhaps one other person who wished to be with you."

"If I had the choice, it would be very difficult

to know who would be the right companion for eternity," Bertilla answered.

Lord Saire smiled to himself.

There was no doubt that if he had suggested the same thing to any other woman of his acquaintance, the answer would automatically have been that she would be completely content if she were with him.

But he knew that Bertilla, puzzling things out in her mind, was when she talked to him completely honest and unselfconscious.

That was why he liked being with her, he told himself, and had found it difficult on several occasions during the last few days not to seek her out.

"Are there many wild animals in Malaya?" she asked now.

"Quite a number," he answered. "Any planter will tell you that tigers are often a serious menace to his labourers, and so are leopards."

"And there are monkeys?"

"The long-tailed macaque monkey will amuse you and so will the flying squirrels."

"I hope I may have a chance of seeing them when I am in Singapore," Bertilla said, "but of course it all depends on when the steamer leaves for Sarawak."

"You shall see them if it is possible for me to arrange a trip up country," Lord Saire promised.

He saw Bertilla's grey eyes light up.

"I would love that!" she said. "It would be wonderful if I could go with you because you know everything and can tell me all the things I want to hear."

Then she said quickly, before he could reply:

"But . . . I do not wish to impose upon you . . . I know how busy you will be when you reach Singapore . . . and you have been so kind to me . . . already."

"I am only glad I was able to help you."

"Lady Sandford has been very kind, and I have enjoyed every moment of the voyage after Alexandria."

She looked up at him with her grey eyes before she said:

"In case I do not get another opportunity, thank you . . . thank you . . . very much indeed for . . . everything!"

"I have already told you, Bertilla, that I do not wish to be thanked."

"But there is no other way I can express my gratitude."

"I hope . . ." he began, then stopped.

What was the point of saying conventionally that he hoped this child would be happy in the future when, if all he suspected about her aunt was true, it would be nothing of the sort?

There was something very sensitive about her, he thought, as she stood looking at the coastline.

The idea of her spending years tending to native children or struggling to get converts to the Christian faith was, he decided, a crime against nature.

Only someone as heartless and selfish as Lady

110

Alvinston could have decided to inflict such an existence on her daughter.

But there was, Lord Saire told himself, nothing he could do about it, and at least Bertilla would have the happiness of this journey to look back on.

Bertilla was actually thinking the same thing.

"I could never forget him," she told herself, "and I shall always remember his kindness, the sound of his voice, and the expression on his handsome face."

She was sure she would never again see a man so handsome and who had so much presence and air of consequence.

'Of course he could do what Sir Stamford Raffles did,' she thought, 'and perhaps do it better. He could lead and command; men would always be ready to follow him because he would inspire them.'

She could understand that women found him irresistible and fell hopelessly in love with him.

When she lay awake in the darkness of the night she would sometimes wonder to herself what he said to them when he made love and what it would be like to be kissed by . . . him. Then she would blush at her thoughts.

Yet it was impossible when she saw him not to feel her heart leap, and now because he was standing close beside her she felt a strange feeling within her breast and a sudden thrill because their elbows, resting on the railing, touched each other.

Lord Saire did not stay with her long, and as

she heard his footsteps receding down the deck Bertilla felt as if her heart went with him.

The day after tomorrow, early in the morning, the ship would dock in Singapore Harbour.

He would say good-bye to her, and although he had said he would try to arrange for her to see the country, she felt that once he was surrounded by the important officials and dignitaries awaiting him at Singapore he would forget about her.

"There also will be beautiful women," Bertilla told herself. "Perhaps he will find them as attractive as he found Lady Gertrude and . . . Mrs. Murray."

She had not actually seen Mrs. Murray because she had left the ship at Alexandria, but she had heard a great deal about her from Lady Ellenton and the attraction she had for Lord Saire lost nothing in the telling.

And there was Daisy, whoever she might be, and a number of other names which kept cropping up in the conversation when the women on the ship talked about Lord Saire as if there was no other subject which interested them.

Even the inevitable gossip about the Prince of Wales and the innumerable ladies who attracted him was not so interesting as the love-affairs of Lord Saire, because they could actually see him and eulogise over his undoubted personal attractions.

Bertilla listened to everything that was said and it did not detract in any way from her admiration for her benefactor. In fact it added to what she already felt about him.

How could it be expected, she asked herself, that any man who was so handsome and so irresistibly alluring would not be pursued by women? And because he was human he would obviously find them attractive too.

It never struck her for one moment that he might be interested in her.

She thought of herself as insignificant and inconspicuous, while Lord Saire existed in a world into which she could never enter.

She was only grateful, like a beggar at his gate, for the crumbs of kindness he might throw her. In her mind he embodied all the heroes of her dreams and those whom she had read about in her books.

As the sun began to sink, the air grew a little cooler, although it was still very hot.

The majority of passengers were far too lazy to rise from their deck-chairs even to look at the coast along which they were steaming.

There were mango swamps and mud flats, rocky shores and coral reefs, while everything else seemed to be covered with trees.

Some of these were heavy with fruit, others flowering spectacularly in brilliant colours which made Bertilla long to see them from close to.

She changed into her evening-gown, then hearing the bugle-call which preceded every meal she went down to dinner, glancing as she entered the Saloon at the table where Lord Saire always sat alone.

The comfort of the First Class Saloon was very different from the cramped communal tables at which the passengers ate in the Second Class.

Here everyone was provided with a comfortable arm-chair, there were potted plants to decorate the corners of the room, and the Band played softly, which gave an irresistible air of gaiety.

The linen-draped tables, the shining cutlery, the bearded stewards who waited silently and most efficiently, were all luxuries, Bertilla thought, which she would never enjoy again.

Because they were coming to the end of the voyage everyone seemed a little more animated than they had been during the heat of the last weeks.

Attractive women like Lady Ellenton had put on their more elaborate gowns and their jewels glittered in the electric light.

When dinner was finished Lady Sandford accepted an invitation to play whist and Bertilla sat for a little while in the Saloon reading a book.

She was longing to go out on deck but she knew it would not be considered correct for her to go alone.

She therefore decided that she would pretend to go to bed; but later, when Lady Sandford and most of the older passengers had retired, she would slip out.

She wanted to look at the phosphorus on the water and the starlight gleaming over the dark trees of the mainland.

There was something mysterious and exciting

about Malaya, Bertilla thought, and if tonight and tomorrow she defied the conventions what did it matter?

Once she was in Sarawak she would never see any of these people again.

She therefore bade Lady Sandford good-night and went to her cabin, not to undress but to sit in a chair reading until she should hear everyone on her passage retiring for the night.

It was not long before she heard doors opening and shutting and cheery voices telling one another: "Sleep well!" and "See you in the morning!"

Bertilla looked at her watch.

It was just after midnight and by now both Lord and Lady Sandford would have retired.

It was so warm that she knew she would not need a coat over her evening-gown, but she took a soft chiffon scarf from the drawer.

It was one of the things which Dawkins had given her from among the "bits and pieces" which belonged to her mother, and she had in fact found nearly all of them very useful.

There were lengths of laces which she had attached to her new gowns, and sashes in different colours so that she could ring the changes and make a dress she had worn several times look different.

There were artificial silk flowers that she could pin onto the bodice of one of the plainer evening-gowns she had made herself.

She draped the chiffon scarf over her shoulders

and looked at herself in the mirror to see if her hair was tidy.

Perhaps, although she dared not count on it, Lord Saire would join her when she was on the top deck as he had done once or twice before.

Then because she heard noise outside which seemed to be growing louder and louder, she opened the door of her cabin and was instantly aware that the passageway was filled with smoke.

She must have gasped with surprise, because in an instant she was coughing and her eyes began to smart.

Hurriedly she ran towards the main landing on which the Purser's Office was situated, and when she reached there she found it crowded with people coming not only from the cabins on the First Class deck but also up the stairs from below.

She saw that a number of them were Chinese, Malayan, and Indian, and she thought they were being driven up because the fire must be in the bowels of the ship.

"Fire!" "Fire!"

The stewards were still shouting the word and now the crew were trying to assemble people into some sort of order on deck.

"Go to the boat-stations!" "Go to the boat-stations!"

Instructions were repeated over and over again.

It was then, as she was being carried along by the sheer pressure of people on either side of her towards a door opening onto the deck, that Bertilla saw ascending the stairs the dark head of Mr. Van da Kaempfer.

Instinctively, because she was afraid of him, she fought her way out of the stream surging onto the decks towards the boats and hid herself in the Coffee-Room.

It was situated on one side of the Purser's Office and was, she saw at a glance, deserted.

She could see through the large port-holes what was occurring on deck and she thought there was no hurry.

If she kept her head and waited, Mr. Van da Kaempfer would go off in one of the first boats and she would not come in contact with him.

The boats were being lowered one after another, and the ship's officers were assisting the women and children into them and seeing that there were also sufficient men to use the oars.

It was all quite orderly and for the moment no-one was panicking, although some of the children were crying and their mothers looked white and anxious.

The noise was shattering, not only from the orders being given by the crew at the tops of their voices, but also because the ship's sirens were sounding and the bells were ringing.

Through the port-holes of the Coffee-Room Bertilla could see that two or three of the boats had drawn away from the ship and in the fading light were moving into the darkness which covered the shore.

"One good thing is that the mainland is not far away," she told herself, "so the boats do not have very far to go."

Everything was happening very quickly, but there still seemed to be people coming up from the lower decks.

Now she heard what sounded like a small explosion and it shook the whole vessel.

'I must get out and find myself a place in a boat,' she decided.

But she had a great reluctance to join the crowd on deck; it seemed safer and less frightening where she was.

Then she saw Lord Saire.

He was still wearing his evening-clothes, so she knew he had not gone to bed.

Like the ship's officers, he was directing passengers into the boats, speaking sharply to one man who tried to push in front of an elderly woman.

He was calm and unflurried, and Bertilla thought as she watched him that he stood out amongst everyone else.

She felt that the people he spoke to trusted him as she did and had confidence that he would see them to safety.

She was so busy watching him as he worked a little way farther down the deck that she was suddenly aware that directly outside the Coffee-Room everyone had gone.

The deck was clear and the officers who had been herding the passengers into the boats were no longer there.

'I must go!' Bertilla thought.

Now she was aware that the ship was listing a little and she had to walk uphill to reach the door.

She went out on deck and as she did so an officer appeared to say almost angrily:

"Where have you been, Madam? All the other ladies have been got away!"

He took her arm and hurried her down to a boat which was just being filled and as they reached it Lord Saire turned and saw her.

"Bertilla!" he exclaimed. "I thought you had gone long ago."

He lifted her up in his arms as he spoke and put her into the boat.

As he did so she saw that behind him the flames were coming out of the port-holes of the Saloon and the smoke made it almost impossible to see the rest of the ship.

"I think that is everybody," the officer said to Lord Saire. "Please get in, M'Lord."

Lord Saire obeyed and the officer got into the boat after him and it was lowered away.

Only as they reached the sea below did Bertilla see that the whole stern of the ship was on fire.

"Pull away! Pull away!" she heard the officer shout.

As the men on the oars obeyed him there was a sudden explosion inside the ship and the whole vessel lurched with the impact of it.

Flames glowing vividly red and gold seemed to shoot up towards the sky; then the *Coromandel* listed to starboard and began to sink lower and lower into the water.

"She's sinking!" a man in the boat growled.

"There's nothing we can do about it," another replied.

"Make for the shore," the officer ordered.

Bertilla realised it was farther away than it had seemed when they were on board.

From water level the darkness of the trees seemed a long way off.

It was growing so dark that although they could hear them, it was difficult to distinguish the other boats making, as they were, for the mainland.

Lord Saire moved along the boat to come and sit beside Bertilla.

"Are you all right?" he asked.

She was so glad that he was with her that for a moment she could think of nothing else, then she answered:

"Quite all . . . right! What . . . happened?"

"I think there must have been an explosion in the engine-room which got out of hand," Lord Saire answered, "but I doubt if we shall ever know exactly what occurred."

He looked to where in a blaze of glory, the flames leaping higher than its masts, the *Coromandel* was going down to oblivion.

"Lord and Lady Sandford are safe?" Bertilla enquired.

"I saw them off myself," Lord Saire answered. "Why were you not with them?"

"The crowds were so pressing," she replied, "and I thought it was foolish to be in a hurry."

"You might have left it too late."

He glanced again towards the burning ship. Bertilla could not say that she had been watching him and had known instinctively that if he was there she would be in no danger.

The men at the oars were moving the boat at a good pace and now they could see ahead of them glittering lights on what must be the beach.

"Where will we land? What will happen to us when we reach the shore?" Bertilla asked.

As if he noticed the sudden nervousness in her voice, Lord Saire turned to smile at her.

"We shall be quite safe," he assured her. "The Malayans are very friendly and as we are so near Singapore there is sure to be someone who will give us a bed for the night."

He spoke confidently, and unexpectedly he put out his hand to take hers.

"You are not afraid, are you?" he asked.

"Not when I am with . . . you," Bertilla replied.

His fingers seemed to tighten on hers and after a moment she said with a touch of laughter in her voice:

"You are rescuing me for the third time . . . but on this occasion it is not my . . . fault."

"Which is doubtless very satisfactory," Lord Saire said, and she knew he was smiling.

The officer gave orders to beach the boat.

The men who were rowing shipped their oars and several of them sprang out to drag the boat a little way up the stony beach.

Passengers from the other boats were already ashore and they could hear their voices in the distance.

A number of Malayans, naked to the waist, appeared, holding, as Bertilla had thought, lanterns, although some had flaming torches.

She waited beside Lord Saire, making no movement until everyone else had stepped onto the beach and the boat was empty. Then he helped her over the thwarts and the ship's officer lifted her out.

The natives with the lanterns were chattering away in a strange language which Bertilla knew was Malayan.

A number of passengers who were with them seemed to be able to understand and even speak it. Chinese passengers were making themselves understood in their own language.

It was now that Bertilla realised she had been the only woman in the boat.

"I think, M'Lord," the ship's officer said to Lord Saire, "these people will find some sort of refuge for yourself and the lady."

As if in answer to his remark, a native speaking halting English said beside them:

"I take — you place — where you — sleep for night."

"Is there a house belonging to a European near here?" Lord Saire enquired.

"I will ask him," the officer said.

He spoke in Malayan and the native replied

with a flow of language.

"He says," the ship's officer interpreted when the man beside him paused for breath, "that the nearest house of any importance where a white man lives is only a mile away if you go through the forest. He will lead you there, but he expects to be paid."

"He will be paid," Lord Saire replied. "Ask him the name of the owner of the house."

The ship's officer obliged, then said:

"The man says the name, as far as I can make out, is something like Henderson."

"That is excellent!" Lord Saire exclaimed. "I know him! Tell the man to guide us through the forest and he will be well rewarded for it."

The ship's officer looked up at the dark trees towering above them.

"Do you think you will be all right, M'Lord?"

"I hope so," Lord Saire answered. "I know these forests are supposed to be almost impenetrable, but the natives always have their own paths."

"That is true," the ship's officer agreed, "but you might be wiser to wait until daylight."

"I think we will risk it," Lord Saire answered.

As if he felt he had been impolite, he said to Bertilla: "That is, if you agree."

"Yes . . . of course," she answered.

The ship's officer explained in Malayan what was required, and holding his candle-lantern at his side their guide set off up the beach.

They followed him, and when they stepped

from the shingle they were immediately in the forest.

The trees grew right down to the shore and huge against the sky seemed very dark and rather frightening.

The Malayan walked ahead, twisting and turning between the trunks of the trees and somehow avoiding the thick shrubs and climbers which appeared to encircle everything.

As if Lord Saire realised it would give Bertilla confidence, and because whatever happened they must not be separated, he reached out and took her hand, leading her as if she were a child.

Her fingers clung to his.

Then as they left the sea behind, all she could see was the light of the lantern and the glimpses it gave her of the trunks and leaves, of blossoms and ferns.

They walked slowly and now Bertilla was aware of what someone had written in a book she had read about Malaya, "the lovely forest perfumes of night."

It was a fragrance like nothing she had ever smelt before and which she knew came from the trees themselves, from their blossoms and the flowers that filled the undergrowth.

On and on they walked and because there was a certain eeriness about it Bertilla felt herself listening.

She could hear the movements of small animals in the undergrowth, the flutter of wings above them as they disturbed birds which had gone to roost or perhaps a flying squirrel which she had longed to see.

She wondered if the monkeys were watching their progress or if perhaps there were even tigers lurking in the darkness.

Her fingers must have tightened instinctively on Lord Saire's, for he stopped for a moment to ask:

"You are all right? We are not going too fast?"

"No, I am quite . . . all right," Bertilla answered.

"You are not frightened?"

"Not with you . . . but I would be . . . alone."

"I will protect you," he said lightly, "but I am afraid the only weapon I have with me is my two bare hands."

"Not very effective against a tiger."

"I am sure our guide could deal with that," Lord Saire replied.

He glanced at the man ahead of them as he spoke and Bertilla saw in the light of the lantern that the Malayan carried a primitive spear in his right hand.

"You see, we have an armed guard!" Lord Saire smiled.

She knew he was reassuring her, and he had known without her telling him that she found the forest ominous and eerie.

She thought how terrified she would have been of the fire on board if Lord Saire had not been with her. Worst of all, Mr. Van da Kaempfer might have constituted himself her protector.

But she was safe with her hand in Lord Saire's and she thought how lucky she was. What was more, she was alone with him as she had never expected to be.

"After all," she said aloud, "this is a very exciting adventure and perhaps one day it will be recounted in your biography."

"You are still envisaging that I shall become famous enough to deserve one."

"Of course you will!" she said. "Perhaps they will relate how you walked in the Malayan jungle and killed a tiger with your bare hands, thereby saving a great number of people from an untimely death."

He laughed and the sound seemed to ring out in the silence of the forest.

"You are determined to make me a hero," he said, "and as it is a position I rather enjoy I shall not try to prevent you."

As he spoke, the trees began to thin and a moment later they saw lights ahead of them.

"Henderson — House!" their guide said, pointing with his finger.

Now he started to move quicker as if anxious to receive the money which had been promised to him.

As they drew nearer, Bertilla could see that the house was in fact a very large bungalow with a sloping roof of green tiles.

Although it was late at night there seemed to be lights in almost every window and as they reached the garden she saw a long verandah running the whole length of the house.

Bertilla wondered if there was a party in progress and she suddenly felt self-conscious about her appearance.

She was still wearing the simple gown she had worn for dinner and had the chiffon scarf over her shoulders.

But her hair had caught in the branches of the trees as they walked through the forest, and she suspected the hem of her gown was stained and her slippers were dirtied by the grasses of the forest path.

She looked at Lord Saire and thought that in his evening-clothes he might have just stepped out of a London Ball-Room.

'I hope he is not ashamed of me,' she thought.

Then they were on the verandah and their guide was hammering loudly on an open door.

There was the sound of voices inside the house and she heard someone say:

"Who on earth can it be at this hour of the night?"

Then a man in a white suit with grey hair and a sunburnt face appeared at the door, carrying a glass in his hand.

Lord Saire moved forward.

"Mr. Henderson!" he exclaimed. "We have not met for some years, but I am Lord Saire. The ship in which I was due to arrive in Singapore has just sunk in the Malacca Straits."

"Good God!" Mr. Henderson ejaculated, and putting out his hand he added: "Of course I remember you, Lord Saire. We met with the Governor. Did you say your ship has sunk?"

"The *Coromandel* has gone down in flames but everyone aboard has been saved."

"Well, thank heavens for that!" Mr. Henderson said. "Come in!"

"May I introduce Miss Bertilla Alvinston, a fellow-passenger," Lord Saire said.

Bertilla put out her hand and Mr. Henderson shook it heartily.

Lord Saire turned back to give their guide several gold coins, then they were being taken into a long comfortable Sitting-Room in which there were six other people sitting about, drinking.

Mrs. Henderson was a plump, smiling, middle-aged woman who exuded good-humour and kindness with every breath she drew.

The guests were obviously planters, like their host.

They plied Lord Saire with questions and made horrified exclamations as he explained what had happened.

"Where will everybody else have gone?" Mrs. Henderson asked.

"There are a number of houses where they could be accommodated," her husband replied, "the Franklins, the Watsons, they're all as near to the sea as we are."

"I dare say most of the passengers would be too nervous to walk through the forest at night," Lord Saire said. "When I asked which was the nearest house, they told me it was yours, and I therefore took the risk of coming to you in the dark."

"I'm very glad you did," Mrs. Henderson smiled.

She rang for servants who produced food and drink for Lord Saire and Bertilla.

There was so much talk and so much excitement over their arrival that it was only after they had been there an hour that Bertilla began to feel sleepy.

Mrs. Henderson noticed it.

"What you need, my dear," she said, "is a good night's sleep."

"I am afraid we possess nothing but what we stand up in," Lord Saire said before Bertilla could answer.

"We can provide you with everything," Mrs. Henderson said, "and you know as well as I do, Lord Saire, that our tailors in Singapore are the quickest in the world. We'll have you both fitted out with new clothes as good as anything you can buy in London within twenty-four hours."

"I hope you are right," Lord Saire said, "I have no desire to call on the Governor in evening-dress!"

"We'll not let you down," Mrs. Henderson promised.

But as Bertilla followed her to where she could sleep, she could not help wondering how she would be able to pay for her clothes with the very little money she had with her.

Bertilla awoke to find the sun pouring in through the windows of the very attractive bed-room which looked out over the garden.

As she went to the window, she was excited at seeing for the first time in her life great beds of orchids.

She had seen her mother going out to dinner wearing orchids on her shoulder, and a bride carrying them at a fashionable wedding.

But never had she expected to see thousands of them in every colour, growing in flower-beds, and to know that if her guide-book was right they also grew wild all over the country.

She was wondering if she would be obliged to put on her evening-dress to go down to breakfast when a maid appeared with a gown.

It belonged, she was told, to Mrs. Henderson's daughter, and it fitted perfectly except it was a little too large round the waist.

It was much more expensive and attractive than any of Bertilla's gowns, and having arranged her hair she hoped that Lord Saire would not be ashamed of her.

When she was ready she went somewhat shyly towards the verandah where she was told her host and hostess would be breakfasting.

She found that Lord Saire, like herself, had borrowed some day-clothes, and in a white tussore suit he looked somehow different.

"We've already sent to Singapore for tailors," Mrs. Henderson said after she had greeted

Bertilla, "and all you have to do now is to go shopping without having to enter a shop. I must say it's one of the things I enjoy most about living in the East."

"I am afraid I cannot . . . afford anything at all . . . expensive," Bertilla said, remembering that she had to pay her Hotel accommodation before she left for Sarawak.

"If you are worried about that," Lord Saire said, "I am quite certain we shall all be fully compensated for what we have lost by the Steamship Company."

He smiled at her encouragingly and added:

"The only trouble is that we shall have to wait during all the arguments there will be over the insurance; so in the meantime, Bertilla, you must allow me to be your Banker."

"It is very . . . kind of you," Bertilla replied, "but . . ."

She thought it would be difficult to explain in front of the other people present that she did not wish to once again be an encumbrance upon him.

But before she could speak Mrs. Henderson interposed:

"Now you're not to worry about little things like that, Lord Saire. I am going to look after Miss Alvinston — or rather, Bertilla — if she will allow me. It's a long time since I have had the pleasure of dressing a daughter. Mine has been married for five years, so this is going to be my welcome-present to a new visitor to Singapore."

Bertilla tried to protest, but Mrs. Henderson swept all her arguments to one side.

"It's what I want to do," she said, "and my husband'll tell you that when I set my heart upon anything there's no gainsaying me."

Bertilla thought later that it was fascinating to have the tailors, who were all Chinese, arriving with roll upon roll of different materials which they spread out on the verandah for her inspection.

There were satins, lamés, and embroidered silks in a dozen different designs, each more attractive than the last.

Bertilla felt she would never have been able to make up her mind, but Mrs. Henderson knew exactly what she wanted.

She gave her orders with a sharpness and a precision about which there could be no misunderstanding.

"Please . . . please . . . no more," Bertilla cried over and over again, but her hostess had no intention of listening to her.

"I shall never be able to wear all these gowns in Sarawak," she said at last, despairingly.

"In Sarawak?" Mrs. Henderson exclaimed. "Why are you going to Sarawak?"

"I am to live with my aunt," Bertilla explained.

"Well, I must say you're full of surprises!" Mrs. Henderson said. "I should not have imagined you would want to live in such an isolated place at your age."

"I had no choice in the matter."

"From all I hear, it's very dull in Sarawak, but you will at least have some pretty clothes to console you," Mrs. Henderson said. "I'm sure there's no hurry for you to get there, so Singapore can enjoy seeing them before you leave."

Bertilla did not know what to say to that.

She had a feeling that if she behaved as she ought to she would leave for Sarawak as soon as possible.

But she obviously could not go without a single thing to wear except the evening-gown in which she had arrived, and which, as she had expected, had suffered from her walk through the forest.

"Leave everything to me," Mrs. Henderson said, and for the moment Bertilla was only too happy to do as she was told.

At luncheon-time she learnt that Lord and Lady Sandford were quite safe and had been moved from the very uncomfortable shelter in which they had spent the night to a planter's house a few miles away.

"I have sent them a message to say that we are here and very well looked after," Lord Saire told Bertilla.

"I am glad," she answered. "I would not want Lady Sandford to worry about me."

"If you had behaved correctly you should have gone with her when the fire started," Lord Saire said.

But he was smiling as he spoke, and Bertilla knew it was not really a rebuke.

"I much preferred to be with you . . ." she said honestly, "and Mrs. Henderson is very kind."

"In case you are worrying about what she is spending on you," Lord Saire said in a low voice, "let me assure you that the Hendersons are very rich and they can afford to be generous."

She gave him a quick smile which told him that she appreciated that he was thinking of her feelings.

He thought that despite the elegance of the gown she had borrowed and her smile, there was something pathetic and a little lost about her.

It was the first time in his life that he had ever felt an urge to protect a woman or keep her from feeling embarrassed or uncomfortable.

In the past if anyone needed protection it had been himself!

The goddesses like Gertrude and his other loves had all been fully capable of looking after themselves and getting everything they wanted in the world by sheer determination.

In a way, despite the femininity of their appearance, they were Amazons, women who were ready to fight for everything they desired.

Bertilla, he thought, was very different.

It was not only when she was clearly afraid that he felt anxious to reassure her; it was because she always seemed too small and too unsure of herself to manage alone.

He knew, as she looked away from him over the sunlit garden, that she was trying to avoid being, as she put it, an encumbrance on him.

Any other woman finding herself in such circumstances would have been demanding his attention, giving orders, expecting them to be obeyed, and insisting at the same time on being flattered and inevitably the centre of everybody's attention.

He knew that Bertilla was anxious to draw as little attention to herself as possible.

Yet he noticed that because she was so attentive and because she listened not only with her ears but also with her mind, people were anxious to talk to her and obviously enjoyed her company.

"Bertilla is a very sweet girl, Lord Saire," Mrs. Henderson said later in the evening when Bertilla had gone up to her room to lie down.

"She is very young and all this is rather bewildering for her," Lord Saire said.

"She's not so young that she does not think and feel," Mrs. Henderson answered, "and she also appreciates everything that is done for her. That's unusual today, when most people, young and old, seem to take everything for granted."

That was exactly what the women whom he had known in the past had done, Lord Saire thought.

"What's all this nonsense about the girl going to live in Sarawak?" Mrs. Henderson asked.

"I understand that her mother, Lady Alvinston, is sending her out there to live with her aunt."

Mrs. Henderson looked at Lord Saire.

"You're not referring to Agatha Alvinston by any chance?"

"I believe that is her name."

"Good Lord! Bertilla will have a terrible time with that old harridan! She comes to Singapore occasionally to make trouble and extort money from those who are willing to give her anything as long as she will go away!"

Mrs. Henderson paused, then she said:

"I remember now Sir Charles Brooke saying something about her when he was dining with the Governor last year. We were at a dinner-party and someone — I cannot remember who it was — made a remark about the Missionaries."

"I am sure they are a nuisance in this part of the world," Lord Saire interposed.

"It was worse than that, and they were speaking specifically about Miss Alvinston. I wish I could remember what was said, but it's gone out of my head."

Lord Saire did not speak and after a moment Mrs. Henderson went on:

"You ought to stop Bertilla from going to Sarawak and wasting her life trying to convert a lot of head-hunters who are perfectly happy as they are."

Lord Saire smiled.

"I am afraid Bertilla is not my responsibility, though naturally I am sorry that that is to be her fate."

Mrs. Henderson rose rather heavily from the chair in which she had been sitting.

"She may not be your responsibility at the moment, Lord Saire," she said, "but if you take my advice you'll make it yours."

She walked out of the room as she spoke, leaving Lord Saire staring after her in astonishment.

After a moment he rose from his chair to pour himself a drink.

Chapter Five

Lord Saire looked round the room and saw no sign of Bertilla.

It was however crowded with a large number of the Hendersons' friends who had been invited especially to meet them.

Some of their near neighbours had also arrived with the passengers from the *Coromandel* who had become their unexpected guests.

There were, therefore, quite a number of familiar faces, and although Lord and Lady Sandford were not among them Lady Ellenton was.

The planters in Malaya were a cheerful lot and the laughter was hearty and unrestrained.

By this time in the evening everyone was getting somewhat merry on the popular local drink known as "Planter's Punch."

It had a basis of rum, but it contained also a local brandy and the mixed juices of the fruits which grew in such profusion, especially pineapple.

A number of the guests were dancing in an adjacent room where a large and very noisy woman was playing the piano.

She sang at intervals while everybody joined in, and the dancing itself grew progressively wilder as the evening wore on.

Lord Saire walked out onto the verandah to find that it was crowded too and above the noise and the laughter there was the continual shout of "Boy!" for a servant to bring more drinks.

He had the feeling that Bertilla would be somewhere in the garden, seeking an isolated spot as she had done on the ship.

After moving between the orchid-beds and beneath the trees of frangipani heavy with blossom, he found her.

She was looking out over the countryside, which gleamed white and mysterious in the light of the moon.

Her gown, which was one of the new ones made for her within the twenty-four hours that Mrs. Henderson had promised, was, Lord Saire had thought when she came down to dinner, very attractive.

Always before he had seen her very simply and almost drably dressed. But the gown which Mrs. Henderson had chosen was swept back into an elegant bustle.

There were bunches of artificial pink roses on either side of it and the same flowers decorated the low bodice.

It was a gown that any London débutante

would have been pleased to wear and Lord Saire had known as Bertilla entered the room that her eyes sought his and asked him wordlessly if he approved.

He had noticed since their arrival at the Henderson House that she continually sought his approval of something she had said or done.

Not by asking him awkward questions and expecting compliments, as another woman might have done, but just questioning him with her grey eyes, and knowing by the expression in his what was the answer.

"She needs looking after," Lord Saire had said to himself not once but a hundred times.

Yet he told himself that it would be a great mistake for him to become too involved in Bertilla's future: he certainly had no authority to suggest any alternative to her living with her aunt in Sarawak.

He could not help thinking that there must be some way in which she could earn her living in Singapore.

But he had no idea what that could be and he had no intention of taking Mrs. Henderson into his confidence.

He had an unmistakable feeling that she was match-making where he and Bertilla were concerned, and he told himself irritably that it was impossible for him even to speak to a woman without someone expecting wedding-bells.

Nevertheless, he found himself thinking continually of Bertilla and her problems, and he noticed that in the happy, genial atmosphere of Henderson House she seemed to blossom like one of the flowers in the garden.

He found himself watching for the light in her eyes, the smile on her lips, and the way she seemed to be losing some of the insecurity which had been so obvious when he talked to her before.

"It is that damned mother of hers," he told himself, "who has made her afraid of everything and everybody!"

He thought once again that she was like a puppy, ready to trust everyone, until she found that blows and harsh words were to be expected rather than kindness.

He knew as he now saw Bertilla silhouetted against the flowering shrubs and the frangipani trees that he had been half-afraid that she might be encountering difficulties with one of the planters.

He had noticed during dinner and afterwards how eagerly the younger men sought out her company.

He knew that anyone as lovely as Bertilla would be an excitement and inevitably a temptation in a land where young and pretty English women were few and far between.

He remembered the fear that had been in her eyes when she told him about the Dutchman on board the *Coromandel*, and he was determined that if he could prevent it there should be no repetition of what had happened to her then.

Although he was walking very quietly on the grass she must have sensed his approach, for she turned her head before he reached her and now in the moonlight he saw the smile on her lips.

"I wondered where you had disappeared to," he said.

"It is so lovely out here," Bertilla answered. "Could anything be more beautiful?"

"There are a lot of gentlemen back in the house wanting to dance with you."

"I would rather be here, especially now that you . . ."

She did not finish the sentence, as if she felt she was being too personal, and after a moment Lord Saire said:

"I wanted to tell you that tomorrow I am leaving early with Mr. Henderson to inspect his plantation. He owns a great deal of land and it will take us the whole day to see it all."

He paused before he said:

"Henderson has put down a lot of new crops which have never been grown in Malaya before and I want to see the results."

He was telling her exactly what he was doing because he thought that after what he had said about showing her the countryside she might be disappointed that she was not included in to-morrow's expedition.

But it was, as a matter of fact, entirely a business trip, and what he saw would be incorporated in his report which would be sent back to England.

Bertilla did not speak and after a moment he said:

"There will be another day, I am sure, when I can ask you to come with me."

Bertilla looked away from him as she said in a very low voice:

"How long can I . . . stay? Perhaps I should . . . leave for Sarawak."

"I expected you to ask me that," Lord Saire replied. "There is no hurry, Bertilla. Mrs. Henderson has said over and over again how much she likes having you here."

"She has been very kind."

"You will find that the people in Malaya are kind, and they expect their guests to stay for a long time," Lord Saire explained. "Therefore, what I was going to suggest to you was that you should avail yourself of the Hendersons' hospitality for several weeks at least."

"Could I do . . . that?"

He heard the excitement in her voice.

"Why not?" he asked. "I do not intend to move to Government House until my wardrobe is fully replenished."

"I am afraid you lost much more than your clothes on the ship."

Lord Saire was surprised that Bertilla should be intelligent enough to know that his notes, his books, and a great number of other papers were an irreplaceable loss.

Aloud he said:

"Perhaps it is good for me to have to rely on

my memory for a change. Anyone who has a great deal to do with bureaucracy becomes a slave sooner or later to the written word."

"I am sure you will find your mind is just as effective as any memorandum."

"I hope you are right, although I rather doubt it!" Lord Saire smiled.

"When you move to Singapore, how long will you stay there?" Bertilla asked.

He was finding himself unusually perceptive where Bertilla was concerned, and he knew that she was feeling that as long as he was somewhere in the vicinity she had someone to turn to in trouble, someone who in an emergency would protect and save her.

Because he knew it was the answer she wanted to hear, he replied:

"Quite some time, and before I leave this part of the world completely, I intend to visit Sumatra, Java, Bali, and perhaps, who knows, even Sarawak!"

"Is it really . . . possible that you would come . . . there?" Bertilla asked.

"I shall certainly put it on my schedule," Lord Saire promised.

He knew that his answer brought her a sudden happiness and he thought again how very vulnerable she was and how frightening the future must seem to anyone so young and inexperienced.

On an impulse he said:

"When I get to Government House in

Singapore I will speak to the Governor, and see if there is someone with whom you could stay for a short while."

Bertilla gave a little murmur and he continued:

"I know you would like to see how all Sir Stamford Raffles's plans and ambitions have developed thirty years later."

"It would be very exciting to see the harbour and all the buildings I have read about in the book you gave me."

She hesitated, then she added:

"I was . . . expecting to stay in a . . . cheap Hotel while I was . . . waiting for the steamer, but I do not like to ask Mrs. Henderson to recommend one. She has been so kind and generous that it would look as if I was asking her to pay."

"I am quite certain there will be no question of your going alone to a Hotel," Lord Saire said sharply. "As I have already said, Bertilla, people are very hospitable in this part of the world, and I will arrange for you to stay with someone in the town as their guest."

As he spoke, he thought how much he disliked the idea of Bertilla being pushed round from pillar to post and having to rely on the charity of strangers.

At the same time, it was unthinkable for her to stay alone in a Hotel.

'Only Lady Alvinston could have planned anything so diabolical,' he thought, but aloud he said:

"Leave everything to me. I will arrange something — you may be sure of that!"

"Is it possible to find any more words to describe your . . . kindness?" Bertilla asked. "I was thinking last night how inadequate English is as a language in which to express emotion."

"That I believe is true," Lord Saire replied, "but the French are past-masters when it comes to speaking of love."

He spoke lightly and his remark was one which he would have made automatically to any of the women with whom he flirted.

But Bertilla did not respond with the sort of repartee with which he was only too familiar. Instead she said in a forlorn little voice:

"Love is . . . something that I shall never . . . learn about . . . in . . . Sarawak."

"Why should you say that?" Lord Saire asked.

"Because in the book you gave me about the country it said there were very few Europeans there, and those there are, are not . . . likely to be . . . interested in a Missionary."

This was so indisputably true that Lord Saire was at a loss to answer her. But he was surprised that Bertilla should have reasoned the position out for herself.

"Perhaps it will be better than you fear," he said aloud.

She turned to face him, her eyes raised to his as she said:

"I do not want you to think I am complaining. It will be so marvellous for me to have this to . . . remember, when I might have had . . . nothing."

The sincerity in her voice was very moving.

As she looked up at him, the moonlight turning her fair hair to silver, her eyes dark and mysterious in her heart-shaped face, she looked lovely and ethereal.

She was a creature from another world, Lord Saire thought, and without really thinking what he was doing, he put out his arms and drew her close to him.

The magic of the night, the beauty all round them, and his feelings of compassion and tenderness for Bertilla made him forget the caution, prudence, and self-control which were part of his training.

Instead he looked down at her for a long moment, then his mouth was on hers.

His lips were gentle and yet at the same time possessive, as if he tried to capture something that was elusive about her and make it his.

Then as he felt the softness and innocence of her mouth beneath his, as he felt her whole body quiver as if with a sudden ecstasy, his kiss grew more possessive, more passionate.

Yet the tenderness was still there, as if he were touching a flower.

For Bertilla it was as if all Heaven had opened and lifted her into a rapture and glory that was indescribable.

She only knew that this was what she had longed for, yearned for, and yet not really known it could even be a possibility.

At the touch of Lord Saire's arms her whole

body melted into his and she became incredibly and miraculously a part of him.

His lips brought her an ecstasy that she had never known existed, and she felt a sense of wonder and adoration move through her until it was as if everything that was beautiful and everything that she had ever known was divine was there in him.

'This is love!' she thought.

And yet it was so much more, it was everything she had sought and longed for and known in the back of her mind was somewhere, if she could only find it.

It was part of the God in whom she believed, and yet a rapture and excitement that was very human.

How long Lord Saire held her captive they neither of them had any idea.

At last slowly he raised his head to look down into the darkness of her eyes, and as her lips parted he heard her whisper:

"That is the . . . most wonderful . . . the most perfect thing that could ever . . . happen to me!"

Even as she spoke, her voice very soft and yet vibrant with a strange, compelling excitement, there was a sudden shout which seemed to echo all over the garden.

"Saire! Where are you, Saire?"

It was Mr. Henderson calling for his most important guest.

As Lord Saire instinctively stiffened, Bertilla moved from the safety of his arms and slipped away from him into the shadows.

One moment she was there, the next minute she was gone.

Lord Saire realised she would not wish to go back to the house with him feeling, even as he did, that they had fallen from the very peak of an enchanted mountain down into the plains.

Slowly he walked back alone over the lawn towards the house.

He imagined that Bertilla would go to her own room and would not wish to join the noisy merrymaking guests who still thronged the verandah and the Sitting-Room where the music was growing louder.

He was right in that assumption.

Bertilla, after watching him walk back to the house and in the golden light from the windows join his host, went to her own room.

"You have an old friend here," Mr. Henderson's voice boomed out as Lord Saire walked up the steps to the verandah, "who has come out from Singapore to greet you."

Bertilla did not wait to hear any more.

Carefully she edged her way in the shadows round the house until she could enter it by a door at the back and reach her own bed-room without being seen.

She could still hear the sound of voices and the music, but they were faint and unimportant beside the wonder which glowed within her like a lamp that had been lit in the darkness.

She knew now, she told herself, what love was

like, and she knew too that a kiss could be a most ecstatic experience beyond words, beyond description.

"I love him! I love him!" she whispered. "And he has kissed me! He has kissed me and I shall never be the same again!"

She told herself humbly that it could not have meant very much to him, but for her it was a revelation which had come from Heaven itself.

In the future, she thought, when she was alone she would only have to close her eyes to feel his arms around her and his lips on hers.

She felt a paean of happiness well up inside her because, however lonely, however miserable she might be this one perfect thing could never be taken away from her.

It was hers — hers for all time, and if nothing else ever happened in her life she had for her very own a treasure beyond price.

She did not get into bed but sat in a chair, feeling as if she were encompassed round with sunshine and her whole body pulsated in a manner that she could not describe, but she knew it was as if the life-force itself moved within her.

'I love him! I love him and I will worship him in my heart for all time,' she thought.

It never struck her to feel possessive or even for one moment to imagine that she could mean anything special to Lord Saire.

There were so many women in his life, beautiful, exotic women who she imagined would look something like her mother.

They moved in the same distinguished Royal Circle as Lord Saire, where someone as insignificant as herself could never intrude.

He was like a King amongst such women, and they gave him gladly what he asked because he was irresistible.

But for herself Bertilla knew it was very different.

She had nothing to give, and yet in his fineness, in his generosity, he had given her this marvellous happiness when she least expected it.

"He kissed me! He kissed me!"

She hugged the knowledge to herself, feeling it was almost like a child she held in her arms and which belonged to her, and yet he had a part of it.

She sat for a long time remembering exactly what had occurred, feeling the wonder of it in her mind, in her body, and on her lips.

When finally she undressed and got into bed, the house was quiet and the guests must all have left.

Because it was already dawn before she slept, Bertilla awoke to find in consternation that the morning was far advanced.

She knew that Lord Saire would have left the house with Mr. Henderson for their tour of the plantation, and she rose and dressed quickly to apologise to her hostess for being so late for breakfast.

As she looked at her face in the mirror she expected to find it different because of the happiness which surged within her.

She thought there was a new light in her grey eyes and a softness about her mouth that had never been there before.

Because her thoughts enveloped her like a golden haze, she almost hated to leave her bedroom, to have to speak in commonplace tones to ordinary people.

She thought that the sunshine was more golden and the flowers she could see outside in the garden more brilliant than they had ever been before.

She moved from her bed-room, which was at the far end of the house, along the corridor which led to the Reception-Rooms.

Breakfast was usually laid on the verandah outside the Dining-Room and Bertilla was just about to step through the long open windows of the Sitting-Room when she heard her own name mentioned.

Instinctively she came to a standstill.

"What do you think of Bertilla Alvinston?" she heard someone say.

The voice was familiar, then she knew who had spoken — it was Lady Ellenton.

She had been present at the party last night, brought by planters named Watson, with whom she was staying, and she had gushed at Lord Saire in a manner which had made Bertilla feel almost uncomfortable because she felt sure that he disliked it.

"I find her delightful and very good-mannered," Mrs. Henderson replied.

Lady Ellenton gave one of her giggles which Bertilla remembered.

"I cannot help thinking it is funny," she said, "that Lord Saire — the Love Pirate — had to be shipwrecked, which is romantic in itself, not with one of the alluring women with whom he is always connected but with no-one more exciting than an immature girl!"

"I find Bertilla extremely intelligent," Mrs. Henderson said.

"But no-one could call her sophisticated," Lady Ellenton sneered, "and I can assure you from long experience that Lord Saire's *affaires de coeur* are always with very sophisticated women."

"I cannot believe that a ship on fire is a particularly appropriate background for a love-affair," Mrs. Henderson remarked.

Bertilla knew by her tone of voice that she was disliking Lady Ellenton and was on the defensive where her guests were concerned.

But Lady Ellenton giggled again.

"Anyplace, anywhere will do as far as Lord Saire is concerned, and I hear that one of his past loves, Lady Boyner, is waiting for him in Singapore."

"Lady Boyner?" Mrs. Henderson questioned.

"Yes, she and her husband arrived, I am told, only two days ago from India, and she is very attractive. I may tell you, Lord Saire was completely infatuated with her when he was last in Calcutta."

"Well, I'm sure he will be pleased to see an old friend again," Mrs. Henderson remarked.

"He had better get rid of that tiresome encumbrance he has saddled himself with at the moment," Lady Ellenton said. "I know Lady Boyner and she is insanely jealous. It is rumoured that on one occasion she tried to shoot a lover who had turned his attention to some other woman!"

"Good gracious!" Mrs. Henderson exclaimed. "I hope we will not have that sort of thing happening in Singapore!"

"I expect Lord Saire can look after himself," Lady Ellenton replied, "but if he is not careful he will have that creature with fair hair hanging round his neck like a piece of clinging ivy."

"I am quite certain Bertilla will do nothing of the sort," Mrs. Henderson said sharply.

"I hope you are right," Lady Ellenton replied. "But Lord Saire has always seemed to me to be very chivalrous, and chivalry is something which a man can find very costly."

Mrs. Henderson pushed back her chair.

"If you will excuse me, Lady Ellenton," she said, "I will just go and see what has happened to Bertilla. I told the maids to let her sleep, but I imagine she must be awake by now."

She must have moved while she was still speaking, for suddenly she walked from the verandah into the Sitting-Room and saw Bertilla standing just a few feet away from the open window.

One glance was enough to tell the older woman that she had overheard what had been said.

She put her arm round Bertilla's shoulders and drew her to the other side of the room to give her time to recover.

"Take no notice," she said quietly. "She's a spiteful busybody! If you ask me, she's jealous because Lord Saire has paid no attention to her personally."

Bertilla did not answer.

She felt as if her voice was strangled in her throat.

Lord Saire returned later than he had expected and the sun was sinking in a blaze of glory.

As they neared the house Mr. Henderson said:

"I don't know about you, Saire, but I'll be damned glad of a drink. My throat feels like the bottom of a parrot's cage!"

"That might be the result of too much Punch last night," Lord Saire suggested.

"I made it a bit too strong for some of my guests. I imagine a number of them had a hang-over this morning."

"And you?" Lord Saire enquired.

"Nothing affects me," Mr. Henderson boasted. "I was brought up in Scotland, where a man learns to take his whisky at an early age. Then I was in Australia for a few years before I came out here, and that's as good an education for drinking as any man can have!"

"I will take your word for it," Lord Saire replied a little dryly.

He himself was always abstemious and he

disliked men who got drunk whether it was in England or in any other part of the world.

He was well aware that it was the British from Britain who were the heaviest drinkers.

The Australians had a reputation as beer-drinkers and they also produced one or two excellent wines, but he himself preferred, as did all the moneyed classes, champagne.

Champagne had become extremely important to the Empire-Builders and it was the drink of the day.

The Prince of Wales used to tell a story over and over again of how when West Ridgeway, later Governor of Ceylon, marched under Lord Roberts from Kabul to Kandahar, he was haunted throughout the whole journey by the thought of iced champagne.

The Prince would pause then and say:

"Ridgeway told me himself that when Roberts ordered him to ride to the nearest railway station with an urgent despatch, the first thing that occurred to him was that at any Indian railway station iced champagne would be available."

"And was it?" Lord Saire enquired, as was obviously expected of him.

The Prince used to laugh until it started a fit of coughing and when he could speak he said:

"Ridgeway telegraphed ahead to reserve a bottle and rode breakneck for three days and nights — but oh, the disappointment! He said later: 'The ice was melted, the champagne was corked, and the next morning I had a head!'"

Mr. Henderson drew up in front of the house and pulled his tired horses to a standstill.

"Now for our drinks, Saire," he said, "and I think I can offer you anything that you fancy in the way of alcohol."

"If I have a choice," Lord Saire replied, "I would enjoy a glass of champagne."

"It's yours!" Mr. Henderson shouted, "and a damned good vintage at that!"

He hurried ahead of his guest up the steps, shouting to his wife as he did so.

"Muriel! Where are you, Muriel?"

"I'm here," Mrs. Henderson answered, coming out of the Sitting-Room and kissing her noisy husband affectionately on his cheek.

"You're hot and dusty!" she said accusingly.

"What do you expect?" her husband retorted. "We've been miles today, but Saire is extremely impressed by what he saw."

"Very impressed," Lord Saire agreed. "I will go and wash."

"Your champagne'll be ready for you when you return," Mr. Henderson shouted after him, and started bellowing orders to the servants.

Ten minutes later Lord Saire, having changed completely into fresh clothing, was walking towards the verandah.

Cosnet had been located amongst the other passengers from the ship and had joined him two days previously.

It was a relief to have everything ready the moment he needed it, and to allow Cosnet to take over the supervision of the clothes he had ordered from the local tailors.

He knew as well as, if not better than, his master what was required, and Lord Saire's new wardrobe was growing day by day with suits made almost as well as those he had bought in Savile Row.

"Come and sit down, Lord Saire," Mrs. Henderson said with a smile.

He saw that beside the table there was an ice-bucket in which reposed a bottle of excellent champagne.

A servant poured him out a glass and put the bottle back in the ice to cool further.

"Where is Bertilla?" Lord Saire asked.

He sat back at his ease in a deep, comfortable bamboo arm-chair made by the Malayans and lined with a number of silk cushions.

Mrs. Henderson paused for a moment before she said quietly:

"Bertilla has gone!"

"Gone? What do you mean — gone?" Lord Saire enquired sharply.

"There was a boat leaving Singapore for Sarawak at four o'clock this afternoon. She insisted on being on it."

"She insisted? But why? I do not understand."

Mrs. Henderson looked uncomfortable.

"I couldn't prevent her from leaving, Lord Saire. I did my best, I promise you, but she wouldn't listen to me."

Lord Saire put down his glass of champagne.

"Something must have upset her for her to make such a decision."

There was a pause before Mrs. Henderson said even more uncomfortably:

"I'm afraid it was something she overheard."

"Will you please tell me what it was?"

There was a note of command in Lord Saire's voice which Mrs. Henderson had not heard before.

"It was very unfortunate," she began hesitantly, "that Lady Ellenton should have said what she did on the verandah. I didn't know, of course, that Bertilla would be in the Sitting-Room and therefore able to hear every word."

"Lady Ellenton!" Lord Saire exclaimed. "What was she doing here?"

"She came over this morning with Mr. Watson. He left her to have breakfast with me while he went to see our overseer about some plants they were exchanging."

"What happened?" Lord Saire asked.

"Do you wish me to repeat exactly what Lady Ellenton said?"

"I insist that you do so," he said. "Bertilla was in my charge and I cannot understand why she should leave in such a precipitate manner."

"I begged her to stay — I did really!" Mrs. Henderson said. "Quite frankly, Lord Saire, I love that girl. She's the sweetest, gentlest creature, and I wouldn't have had her hurt for the world."

"She was hurt?"

"It was impossible for her not to have been by what Lady Ellenton said."

Lord Saire's lips tightened.

Lady Ellenton was in fact the type of gossipy woman he most disliked.

They were to be found all over the world, but especially in small communities like Singapore.

They managed to do an enormous amount of harm just by talking spitefully and exaggeratedly about everybody and everything which occurred.

"If only I'd had the sense to stop her the moment she mentioned Bertilla's name," Mrs. Henderson said. "But I was being polite. After all, she was a guest in my house, and it was only after the damage was done and Bertilla insisted upon leaving that I thought what a fool I'd been."

"Before we discuss it further," Lord Saire said, "please tell me word for word exactly what Lady Ellenton did say."

Mrs. Henderson drew in her breath and told him.

When she finished there was a long silence. She had been unable to look at him while she was speaking, but now Mrs. Henderson turned her head to see how Lord Saire had taken it.

As she did so she thought to herself:

'It'll doubtless come as a shock to him to know how people talk about him, but it'll do him good! He is far too conscious of his own importance for my liking.'

Lord Saire appeared to be thinking deeply, then he said:

"How did Bertilla know there was a ship leaving Singapore for Sarawak this afternoon?"

"She insisted on finding out when it would be going and my husband has a list of sailings to all the different islands."

"I see . . . then you sent her into Singapore?"

"I took her," Mrs. Henderson corrected. "You do not imagine I would let that poor child go off on her own?"

She looked searchingly at Lord Saire as she added:

"Believe me, I begged and pleaded with her to wait until you returned — in fact I almost went down on my knees — but she wouldn't listen! She wanted to get away, and short of physically keeping her a prisoner there was nothing I could do about it."

"I think I can understand," Lord Saire said slowly.

With a perception that was unusual he understood Bertilla's urgent determination to leave simply because she was so different from any other woman he had met.

What had happened last night had been, as she told him, so wonderful, so perfect that she could not bear it to be spoilt.

Because it would mean something to her for the rest of her life, because it was a rapture she had never experienced before and thought would never happen again, she could not bear to stay.

She was asking nothing of him, expecting nothing, only wishing to keep what she had already untarnished not only from the world but also from him.

It was almost as if he could read her thoughts and feelings.

After what she had heard, thinking she was doing what he would want, she had gone out of his life as unexpectedly as she had come into it.

For the first time for many years Lord Saire looked deeply into himself and was appalled by what he saw.

Once when he had been young and idealistic he had thought of women with respect and they had seemed to him to be precious creatures to whom a man should give both his homage and his allegiance.

He had loved his mother very deeply and she had been everything that he thought a woman should be: gentle, compassionate, understanding.

She had loved his father with a selfless devotion that had made their marriage an idyllic one such as Lord Saire had never found elsewhere.

Their only sorrow had been that their son was an only child and in consequence he had been spoilt.

Because he had found such happiness and perfection at home he had gone out into the world with such high standards that it was inevitable that he should become disillusioned.

He had been at first horrified by the way married women were ready to be unfaithful to their husbands, to give only lip-service to their marriage-vows, and to fall overwhelmingly in love with any man like himself who took their fancy.

He had been horrified, and yet inevitably he had connived at their infidelity and accepted the favours he was offered so freely.

He would have been inhuman if he had not done so.

But at the same time, something within him wept that his idols had feet of clay and that no woman remained long on the pedestal for which by nature she was intended.

Always, he thought now, at the back of his mind he had measured the women with whom he was infatuated by the standards set for him by his mother.

When she died he knew there was a place in his heart that no other woman could ever fill.

Yet after her death he seemed to become more frequently and more easily involved in love-affairs which, fiery and tempestuous to begin with, soon palled and left him once again bored and disillusioned.

He knew now it was because he had been seeking not only the love that his mother had given him and which he missed unbearably, but also the love she had for his father.

This was what he knew he must find if he was to marry and have any chance of happiness.

It was because he was so desperately afraid of making a mistake, of accepting second best rather than a marriage of true love, that he told himself and his friends like D'Arcy Charington that he would never marry.

He could never, he thought, be fortunate enough to find a woman like his mother whose character and personality would bring him what he needed.

A woman who also would love him wholeheartedly, so that there would never be any question of there being another man in her life.

He had so often been the lover of women who had kind and decent husbands.

He had contributed to the break-up of many marriages which were collapsing privately, if not publicly, so he knew only too well what he would abhor and shrink from in his own private life.

"Never," he vowed, "never, never would I marry a woman who could be promiscuous behind my back and deceive me with my closest friends. A woman who would indulge in an intrigue when I was not at her side and be blatantly unfaithful in other people's houses and doubtless, if it suited her, in my own."

Everything that was decent, everything that was idealistic within him, felt revolted when the women who said they loved him sneered or laughed at their husbands.

He also abhorred those who, like Lady Alvinston, turned their backs on their responsibility for their children and the example they should set for them.

All this had combined to make Lord Saire afraid of marriage, afraid of committing himself to an irrevocable way of life which would inevitably end in disaster.

Now, as everything he had done and everything he had felt swept before his eyes, he found himself remembering the kiss he had given Bertilla last evening in the garden.

All night he had felt the softness of her lips and the quiver of her body against his.

He had known that the sensation that had aroused them both had been different from anything he had experienced before.

She was lovely in a different way from any other woman he had ever seen.

But there was something deeper and far more important than the desire she aroused in him or the irresistible passion of his lips.

He had felt something else and he knew that it was in fact sacred, although he was too shy to acknowledge the word.

Bertilla was very young and very inexperienced; at the same time, she had a fundamental sensibility that came not from any physical emotion but from something intensely spiritual.

It would have been impossible, Lord Saire told himself, for him to think or even to imagine such an idea a few weeks ago.

He had given and taken thousands of kisses but there had never been one like that which he had given Bertilla last night, to which she had responded with her whole being.

He knew now that she had given him her soul and that it was a gift he had never been offered before.

At the same time, she had awakened something in him which he had thought was long dead — his idealism.

Once again he saw himself as a Knight riding forth to fight for the purity of a woman and not only to love her because she was human but to worship her because she was Divine.

'This is what I have been seeking all my life,' he thought.

It seemed incredible that it had been there and he had only to put out his hand to touch it, yet he had only realised it was a miracle when it had gone.

Unaware what he was doing or even that he had moved, Lord Saire rose from the chair in which he had been sitting to stand on the edge of the verandah.

"Where are you going, Lord Saire?" Mrs. Henderson asked.

He had been thinking so deeply that he had forgotten she was there sitting beside him.

Now, because he wished to confirm it to himself, he answered her truthfully and positively:

"I am going to Sarawak!"

Chapter Six

Lying awake as the steamer chugged its way through the night, Bertilla could think only of Lord Saire.

She imagined she was close in his arms and felt herself thrill once again as his lips touched hers.

She was not conscious that the cabin, small and rather dirty, was stiflingly hot; she could not for the moment even feel afraid of what lay ahead.

She knew that in leaving the man who had kissed her she left behind her whole heart.

She knew that never again would she fall in love; she was sure she was one of those women who would love once and once only in her life.

She could never again picture in her mind some imaginary husband as she had done in the past, because as far as she was concerned there would forever and always be only one man in the whole world.

"I love him!" she whispered.

As she had told him, the words were utterly

inadequate to express her feelings.

She rose as soon as it was dawn, and washed and dressed as best she could in the tiny cabin, which was piled high with her belongings.

She thought that she had not thanked Mrs. Henderson enough for her kindness and for the enormous amount of clothes that had been packed for her in three leather trunks.

In her wild desire to get away, she could think of nothing but Lord Saire, and that she was, as Lady Ellenton had said so truly, clinging to him and embarrassing him in the process.

"How could he possibly want me?" she asked herself.

And when he moved to Singapore there would not only be the Governor and public affairs demanding his attention, but also the woman he had once loved!

She would be beautiful and sophisticated and would renew for him all he had enjoyed in the past.

She thought of how once again Lady Ellenton had called Lord Saire scornfully "the Love Pirate."

Yet if he had plundered her of her love and her heart, she must seem to him a very small and insignificant little vessel compared with the big ships he had captured in the past and would go on capturing in the future.

"He will forget me," she said decisively, "but I will never, never, if I live to be a hundred, ever forget him!"

All the same, however fraught her feelings were on leaving the man she loved, she could not help being interested as later the following day they drew near to Kuching, which was the Capital and Port of Sarawak.

As she moved about the crowded deck where most of the passengers had slept the night, she found they were many types and nationalities, but mostly Malayan, and they smiled at her in a friendly fashion and she smiled back.

She was not able to converse with them and she was in fact rather glad when an old white-haired trader singled her out.

She was not at all afraid of him, for there was something pleasant and fatherly about him which did not in any way resemble Mr. Van da Kaempfer's approach.

"Is this your first visit to Sarawak, young lady?" he asked.

"It is," she replied, "and I believe it is a very beautiful country."

"Beautiful indeed!" he replied. "But still very primitive, and the people are hard to trade with."

"Why is that?" Bertilla asked.

"Because they're not really interested in money," he replied. "Unlike most of the world, they are happy enough without it."

When Bertilla looked at him in surprise, he said:

"There are areas being cultivated with pine-apples, and roads being built, but there's a long way to go before they learn that we need their gutta-percha and sago."

"Is that all you can buy from them?" Bertilla asked interestedly.

"A few diamonds," the old man answered, "birds'-nests, bêches-de-mer, and bezoar stones, but the majority of the population would rather go head-hunting than grow anything I want."

Bertilla felt herself shudder.

"Are they still . . . cutting off the heads of . . . people?"

There was no mistaking the apprehension in her voice and the old trader smiled kindly.

"You'll be safe enough," he said. "They're not likely to touch a white woman, but you have to understand that head-hunting is part of their lives! It'll take a great many years before the White Rajah or anyone else persuades them to give it up."

Bertilla was silent, wishing absurdly that Lord Saire were there to protect her, and the old trader continued:

"When a young Dyak comes of age, no matter how handsome he may be, the girls of his tribe think little of him until he has at least two or three heads to his credit."

"Two or three . . . heads!" Bertilla repeated in a whisper.

"He can sing his love-songs and dance his war-dances," the trader went on, "but always there comes the question: 'How many heads hast thou taken?'"

"So what do the men do?" Bertilla asked,

knowing it was an unnecessary question.

"They go hunting," the trader replied, "and when a man returns with his trophy, preparations are made for a great feast — the Feast of the Dried Heads."

"But . . . surely the Missionaries can . . . persuade them that it is . . . wrong?"

The trader laughed.

"From what I've seen of the Missionaries, they are more trouble than they're worth. Most of them convert only the foolish who are too afraid to run away from them or those who are crafty and think they've something to gain from the white man."

Bertilla was silent, feeling there was nothing she could say and that once again she was alone in the world with nobody to look after her and no-one to whom she could turn.

"Now don't worry yourself," the trader said as if he realised he had upset her. "You'll find the Dyaks are pleasant people, and look very fine indeed when they wear their waving plumes of war and their shields covered with the tufts of hair taken from the heads of those they have murdered!"

Involuntarily Bertilla gave a little cry, and he added:

"They'll smile at you, wearing coloured beads glittering round their necks and looking for all the world as if butter wouldn't melt in their mouths!"

He certainly had done nothing to allay

Bertilla's fears, and yet when they first turned from the sea into the Sarawak River she felt her whole being uplifted by the broad winding beauty of its pale brown water.

Above it was the Santuborg Mountain, wonderfully shaped and majestic, covered with a thick cloak of trees, and at its foot a soft sandy beach and casmarina trees.

The banks of the river were covered with fruit trees, many of which were in blossom.

There were little villages clamped onto the mud-banks, looking as if the palm-leaved houses had been tumbled from a basket and left exactly where they fell.

There were coffee-coloured women standing naked to the waist deep in the water with long bamboo jars upon their shoulders, and children too young even to walk diving and swimming amongst them like little brown tadpoles.

Along the uncultivated banks were pale green mangroves and behind them rose the jungle with tall majestic trees and monkeys swinging from branch to branch.

It was so lovely that Bertilla drew in her breath and longed to tell Lord Saire about it. She knew that he would understand her feelings and share them.

He loved beauty and it meant something to him as it did to her.

She felt that even though he would never know it he would expect her to be brave and try to understand the people of Sarawak, as he tried to understand those of the different countries with which he came in contact.

They tied up against a primitive quay and there were people crowding down to see the steamer come in and to welcome its passengers whether they knew them or not.

There was a great deal of noise and hurly-burly.

When finally Bertilla found herself going down the gang-plank she saw among the beautiful brown, smiling people milling about below her a tall, gaunt figure whom she recognised instantly.

She thought it would be impossible for her Aunt Agatha not to stand out in any crowd, wherever she might be, but particularly here where she looked like a giant among pygmies, and a very unpleasant, awe-inspiring giant at that.

She had grown grimmer and uglier with age.

It was not only her weather-beaten face that seemed to Bertilla more unpleasant than she remembered, but she had also lost her front teeth, which gave her a strange, almost sinister expression.

"So you have arrived!" she said in the hard, harsh voice that seemed to Bertilla to echo back from her childhood.

"Yes, I am here, Aunt Agatha."

Her aunt made no effort to kiss her or even to shake her hand but merely turned and spoke aggressively to the three porters who were carrying Bertilla's trunks.

Bertilla felt almost ashamed that her trunks were so large and heavy while the little men who were carrying them were so small.

Her aunt was ordering them about in a way which made her feel uncomfortable. Then she said:

"This is the third time I have met the streamer. It is just like your mother not to say the exact date on which you would be arriving."

"I do not think Mama knew that the steamer left Singapore only once every fortnight," Bertilla explained, "and besides that, I was delayed because the ship in which I travelled from England caught fire in the Malacca Straits."

If she had thought to surprise her aunt she was unsuccessful.

"On fire?" Agatha Alvinston said sharply. "Did you lose your clothes? If so I will not be able to provide you with more, you may be certain of that!"

"There is no need for you to provide me with anything, Aunt Agatha," Bertilla replied quietly. "Mrs. Henderson, with whom I stayed when we came ashore, provided me with everything new. It was very kind of her."

"More money than sense, I should have thought," her aunt replied disagreeably.

As they were talking they had walked away from the quay-side and now they were moving along a street with wooden houses on either side of it.

Because they were all down on the quay there

were few people about.

But Bertilla had glimpses of hawkers crying their wares in what seemed to be a bazaar, heard gongs beating in a mosque, and the wailing of a one-stringed instrument.

"That reminds me," her aunt said. "Have you any money?"

"Not very much, I am afraid," Bertilla answered, "but more than I expected, as I did not after all have to stay in an Hotel in Singapore."

"How much?" her aunt enquired.

"I do not know exactly," Bertilla answered. "I will count it when we arrive."

She looked down as she spoke at the hand-bag which she carried.

"Give it to me!"

Agatha Alvinston held out her hand, and Bertilla, surprised but obedient, handed over her bag.

Without slackening her pace her aunt opened the bag and with a few deft movements took out the purse and some notes that Bertilla had put inside it.

She transferred them into the pocket of her cotton gown, then with an almost disdainful gesture gave the bag back to Bertilla.

"I would like to keep a little money for myself, Aunt Agatha," Bertilla said.

She was surprised at her aunt's action and felt that to not own even a penny of money might prove to be an embarrassment.

"You will have no use for money," Agatha

Alvinston snapped, "and if, as I suspect, your mother has no intention of paying for your keep, you will have to work for it — and work hard!"

Bertilla looked at her apprehensively.

"I am short-handed enough as it is," her aunt grumbled, "and you cannot trust these people — not one inch! Having taken all one can give them, they run away into the forest and one never sees them again."

Bertilla could not help thinking they were wise to escape from her aunt, but she was not so imprudent as to say so, and they walked on for a little while in silence.

Now they were out of the town and she could see round her the jungle, and especially the orchids. Even those in the Hendersons' garden had not prepared her for a vast forest illuminated by newly opened orchids.

They were a blaze of glory and some of the trees actually seemed to have turned colour, ranging from pale yellow to mauve, under a covering veil of orchids.

From the boughs hung in garlands yards-long clusters of one species and the ground was carpeted with the tiny delicate orchid-like plants.

Bertilla was hoping to see a honey-bear, which was Sarawak's only dangerous animal, or a mouse deer, hero of many legends.

But she had to content herself with a glimpse of an Angus pheasant.

She was particularly looking out for the hornbill, which she knew with its long yellow beak surmounted by a strange projection of brilliant scarlet was one of the most extraordinary-looking birds in the world.

Some of them, she had read, were the size of turkeys, but the ones she saw in the distance flitting amongst the towering trees were smaller.

But if the birds were an excitement, the large colourful butterflies were an enchantment.

In the forest their colours and the exquisite loveliness of their flight were breathtaking.

Looking round her, Bertilla even forgot that her aunt, ominous and overbearing, was beside her.

"It is lovely . . . absolutely lovely!" she exclaimed, talking to herself.

She felt as if it all had a magic that was part of sight, sound, and sense.

She was startled back to reality by her aunt saying:

"Come along! There is no time for wool-gathering. You have wasted enough of my day as it is already."

They walked on for another half a mile and Bertilla was beginning to feel very hot when they came at the end of the road to what she knew at first sight must be the Mission House.

It was long and low, built of wood, and should have been as attractive as the natives' houses which she had seen coming up the river.

Instead, it was ugly and unprepossessing!

The ground in front of it had been stamped by children's feet until the grasses and the exquisite wild flowers that bloomed everywhere else were lost and it appeared to be just a playground of flat mud.

There were three young women, wearing shapeless cotton dresses over their naked bodies, who appeared to be supervising a number of small children.

Until Agatha Alvinston appeared, they were sitting comfortably at their ease, smiling as if at their secret thoughts.

The children were rolling and tumbling about, the majority of them somehow divested of their clothing so that their little dimpled brown bodies were naked.

As Bertilla and her aunt came in sight, a sudden transformation took place.

The three women jumped to their feet and started to shout at the children and scold them.

The laughter died away as the children stopped playing and stood looking frightened.

As soon as Miss Alvinston was within earshot she began berating the women, speaking a language which Bertilla could not understand, but there was no possibility of mistaking the sense of what she said.

She was scolding and at the same time threatening them, Bertilla thought.

They accepted what she had to say without answering back, but merely looked at her with their brown velvet eyes that were like pansies, until finally her voice stopped and she flounced away from them towards the house.

The Mission, Bertilla could see as she got

nearer to it, was very roughly built and was in its construction little more than a large hut.

It was divided into one big room which she thought must be the Class-Room and beyond it were the rooms that would be occupied by her aunt and herself.

It was all very austere and there was nothing in the least cosy or home-like about it.

In fact, from the moment Bertilla entered the building she felt it was a place where love had never been known, and where the atmosphere was unpleasant.

She told herself quickly that she was being foolish to let first impressions have such effect upon her and she should be grateful that her aunt was giving her, if nothing else, a home when no-one else wanted her.

"I suppose you will have to have this bed-room," Agatha Alvinston said grudgingly.

She showed her into a tiny room just large enough to hold a native bed of wood and webbing on which there was a thin, almost nonexistent mattress.

"I have been using it when anyone was sick," she said, "but there is nowhere else for you to sleep."

"I am sorry to cause you such inconvenience, Aunt Agatha."

"So you should be. I suppose now that your Aunt Margaret is dead your mother does not want you. She was always one to shirk her responsibilities."

She spoke in such a disparaging tone that Bertilla longed to fly to the defence of her mother even though she herself secretly thought the same thing.

She knew, however, that there was no point in arguing with her aunt, and so she said nothing.

The Malayans who had carried her trunks all the way from the quay now brought them into the bedroom and put them down on the ground.

"Will you please pay the men, Aunt Agatha," Bertilla said. "You have all my money."

Her aunt immediately entered into what she realised was a long and violent argument as to how much the men should be paid.

As it had been a long and tiring walk and they had each carried one of her trunks on their back, Bertilla wanted to reward them handsomely.

But as she had not a penny left there was nothing she could do but stand by helplessly while her aunt obviously beat them down until they left looking disparagingly at what she had given them with a sullen expression on their faces.

"You had better take off your finery and put on something sensible in which to work," her aunt said.

"Do you think I could have something to drink first?" Bertilla asked. "As it is so hot, I am rather thirsty."

"You can help yourself, but do not expect me to wait on you."

"No, of course not," Bertilla answered. "If you will just show me where things are kept."

She was to find later in the day an explanation for her aunt's gaunt appearance. There was very little food.

She learnt that the children who came to the Mission to be given Christian teaching and education were fed at midday with the cheapest sort of rice.

It was augmented with fruit that could be picked in the jungle and occasionally a little sugar.

The fruits were all strange to Bertilla but she recognised the durian by its horrible smell, which seemed like a combination of onion sauce, cream cheese, and brown sherry.

About the size of a coconut, covered all over with short stout spines, it had a cream-coloured pulp inside it divided into five cells.

Because Bertilla was hungry she forced herself to eat one, and found that it tasted rather like a rich buttered custard.

Her aunt ate the same, and Bertilla, because she was so hungry, forced herself to swallow the rice even while she realised it was an inadequate diet.

There was a type of tea grown locally of which her aunt drank a great many cups a day, and she was told that they would occasionally kill one of the small chickens, little larger than bantams, which ran round the Mission.

It was one of her tasks to find their eggs where they had laid them in the grasses and flowers which grew outside the patch beaten down by the children.

What horrified Bertilla more than anything else was her aunt's attitude towards her helpers.

They were beautiful young women with exquisite figures and long dark hair hanging below their waists. When her aunt was not looking they talked and laughed with one another.

They were obviously full of a natural happiness that bubbled over even in the most adverse circumstances.

One was obviously a Dyak, as she had greatly enlarged ear-lobes from the heavy ear-rings the women usually wore.

The other two, Bertilla thought, were Malayans.

Her aunt left her no illusions about them from the very first evening of her arrival.

Bertilla had come from the Mission House, where she had been told to clean the floor and tidy up after the children had left at the end of the day, and had seen to her horror her aunt striking the Dyak woman across the shoulders with a stick.

She hit her several times, and the woman, screaming loudly, ran away into an adjacent hut made of palm-leaves, where Bertilla had learnt all three women lived.

Agatha Alvinston had shouted something after her which sounded, to say the least of it, unpleasant. Then she had looked round to meet Bertilla's horrified eyes.

"You were . . . striking her, Aunt Agatha!"

"I was! And you will see me do it again and

again," her aunt replied.

"But why? Are you allowed to do it?"

"Allowed? I am allowed to do anything I like with such riff-raff! They should be in prison, but instead they are serving their sentences by working for me."

Bertilla began to understand why the women stayed.

She had already thought that the manner in which her aunt spoke to them would have led any servant at home, let alone a teacher, to hand in her notice at once.

"You say they should be in prison?" she questioned. "What have they done?"

"Stolen, broken the laws, although there are not many of them here to break," Agatha Alvinston answered. "They have to be punished for their sins, as everyone who is a sinner is punished."

She looked at Bertilla in an unpleasant manner as she spoke and Bertilla remembered how when she was a child her aunt was continually exhorting her father to beat her.

She turned away, disgusted and feeling degraded by the manner in which her aunt was behaving.

Later in the evening when she listened to Agatha Alvinston describing her methods of teaching Christianity, she felt even more appalled.

The next day, after she had been fortunate enough to find a nest of eggs hidden under a clump of crimson rhododendrons, she was allowed a small egg for her breakfast.

The children returned to the Mission House and Bertilla saw an example of her aunt's ideas on education.

First there were long and lengthy prayers read by Agatha Alvinston with everybody on their knees. Then there was Bible reading, which seemed to go on interminably.

Then a hymn was sung in English by children who could not understand it and by their so-called teachers who mispronounced every word.

Even so, Bertilla thought they enjoyed the music played by Aunt Agatha on a very old, wheezy portable piano that she was instructed to clean daily against damage that could be done to it by white ants.

After this, three of the children who were old enough were required to repeat their catechism. This usually ended, Bertilla was to discover, in tears and spankings.

Religion was then disposed of until long prayers were repeated parrot-wise before they dispersed in the afternoon.

The three women were expected to teach the children to read simple words and to add.

Coconuts, stones, and pieces of wood were brought for the lessons in adding and Bertilla noticed that as soon as her aunt's back was turned the teachers would lose interest and the children began to play.

There was a disagreeable incident first thing in the morning when the Dyak woman came into the Mission House with a spray of orchids arranged in her dark hair.

The flowers looked very pretty and Bertilla could not help thinking that the woman, who was indeed little more than a girl, looked like a flower herself.

But the mere fact that she had tried to improve her appearance sent her aunt into a fury.

She screamed with rage, tore the flower from the girl's head, pulling out several hairs as she did so, and stamped it on the ground.

She then produced her stick and started to beat the girl over the shoulders as Bertilla had seen her doing the evening before.

It was all rather shaming and undignified, and Bertilla felt so embarrassed that she walked out of the room and went to the other part of the house.

Even there she was unable to escape her aunt's ranting and roaring.

"She is not normal," she told herself. "I think living here alone has sent her mad!"

Then frantically she realised there was no-one she could turn to, no-one she could ask for help.

Because she was so nervous when they had their midday meal together after ladling out the rice for the children, she asked her aunt:

"Are there any Europeans in Kuching?"

"There is the Rajah and his wife," Agatha Alvinston replied sourly, "but they do not understand the work I am doing here and in my opinion he is a man who is not fit for his responsibilities."

"What do you mean by that?" Bertilla asked.

"I have actually with my own ears heard Sir Charles say that English is an uncouth, barbarous language, hardly worth speaking, and he prefers French or the strange gutturals of the Dyaks," Miss Alvinston replied.

She spoke as if French was something unclean and went on:

"You want to know if there are any Europeans? Well, there is a French valet in the Rajah's service, if you would like to associate with him; there are three married couples for whom I have no use, and five or six bachelors who will not come courting you."

"I had not thought of such a thing," Bertilla expostulated.

"Riff-raff! Stupid, ignorant people who do not worship God and are prepared to leave these heathens to their own barbarous and abominable customs!"

Agatha Alvinston's voice rose as she got up from the table to shout:

"I am alone! There is only me — me to carry the word of God and to bring the light of His ways into the darkness."

The way she spoke and what seemed almost like a fire in her eyes made Bertilla even more afraid of her.

'She really is crazy!' she thought, and wondered if she should tell Sir Charles Brooke about it at Astana Palace, where he lived.

Then she told herself that the Rajah who

reigned over the whole of this land would not wish to be worried with her and her troubles.

In such a small community they must all know her aunt and the work she was trying to do. Perhaps someone would come to the Mission and she would have a chance of telling them what she feared.

But no-one came near them. They seemed to live in isolation in the ugly house with its mud-patch playground surrounded almost entirely by jungle.

There were no books in the Mission except for the Bible and a certain number of religious tracts which were sent out regularly from England and which had accumulated from the time her aunt had first come out to Sarawak.

When Bertilla was alone at night lying on her hard bed, she began to feel afraid that she was in a prison from which she could never escape.

She was almost too busy in the daytime to think; for when her aunt had said she intended her to work she had not exaggerated.

Bertilla found she had to clean the whole of the living-quarters of the Mission House and on the second day after her arrival the cooking was turned over to her.

The elderly woman who prepared the rice for the children had either taken ill or had run away.

The floors had to be scrubbed daily because of the encroachment of ants and a great number of other insects which to Bertilla were abhorrent.

There were also the children's clothes — what

187

there were of them — to be washed.

Bertilla discovered that as most of them came to school naked, her aunt had cotton garments made like sacks which they could slip over their heads to hide their dimpled brown bodies.

Because the three prison women did as little as possible and even tried to defy her aunt, Bertilla soon found that it was easier for her to do herself what chores had to be done than to hear her aunt screaming at them and watch her beating them.

It was only at night that she could escape from the noise, the disagreeableness, and the tasks, which seemed to be endless.

Then she would lie alone in her airless little room and listen to the chorus outside of bull-frogs, tree-frogs, and strange beetles, each of which made a noise all their own.

Often she would hear the chorus of sound swell and multiply until it seemed to Bertilla as if every tree and every leaf and every blade of grass was alive and calling into the velvet darkness of the night for its mate.

She knew as they called that she called too, and her heart went out over the sea to a man who had given her all the happiness she would ever know.

"I love him!" she whispered. "I love him and I always will."

It was a week after Bertilla had arrived at the Mission House that she had an experience which left her trembling and afraid.

Two of the older children had been quarrelling and had started to fight, clawing at each other's hair. Yet Bertilla was sure it was more in fun than in anger.

But coming out onto the playground her aunt had taken a different view of it and had started to scream furiously at the Dyak woman, who was in charge.

She worked herself into a frenzy of anger, screaming abuse, then inevitably beating her with the thin stick that was never far from her hand.

The woman turned to run away, and unaccountably, or perhaps she was pushed, fell down.

She was therefore at the mercy of Agatha Alvinston and as she struggled and writhed on the ground the stick fell violently and continuously on her shoulders, on her head, on her back, in fact on every part of her body.

She was so much smaller than the tall, elderly Englishwoman that Bertilla thought it was almost as if she saw her aunt beating one of the children.

Instinctively, hardly realising what she was doing, she ran forward.

"Stop, Aunt Agatha!" she cried. "Stop it at once! It is too much, it is cruel, you have no right to hit anyone like that."

Her aunt appeared not to hear her and in an obvious frenzy she went on striking the fallen woman.

"Stop!" Bertilla cried again.

Then as she put out her hands to catch hold of her aunt's arm, the stick came down on her own shoulders, and having struck her twice her aunt pushed her out of the way and continued punishing the woman on the ground.

The respite had gained the Dyak woman the chance to get to her knees, and now, still enduring the whipping which was making her scream at the top of her voice, she began to crawl away.

Bertilla had also fallen when her aunt pushed her.

Now on the ground, she watched the woman who had got up on her feet running towards the sanctuary of the hut which she shared with the two other teachers.

Suddenly in the thick bushes behind the hut Bertilla saw a face.

It was the face of a man and there was no need for her to be told he was a Dyak.

She could see the blue tattooing on his body and the plumes in his dark hair.

But she had only a glimpse of him, his face contorted with anger. Then the leaves of the bushes closed round him.

Later, when her own back was aching from the few blows her aunt had inflicted on her and she thought with commiseration of how much agony the other woman must be suffering, she wondered if she should tell her aunt what she had seen.

It was the first time since she had come to the

Mission that there had been any sign of a native man.

She could not help thinking it was strange that the women stayed and endured the treatment that was meted out day after day.

This whipping had been more severe than any that she had seen before, and that night Bertilla found it hard to recapture the magic sounds of the frogs and beetles.

She had thought that they were the only inhabitants of the jungle round them.

But now she knew there were Dyak warriors, whose most valued possessions were the dried, smoked heads of those they had decapitated.

Lord Saire arrived in Kuching in a gun-boat.

He had realised that he would have to wait a fortnight after Bertilla had left for the steamer which plied between Singapore and Kuching.

This he had no intention of doing if it could possibly be avoided.

As part of his mission was to meet the Captain of any of the war-ships based at Singapore, it was easy for him to ask for a gun-boat to carry him to one of the islands.

He knew it had caused some surprise that Sarawak was first on his list.

There was a certain amount of trouble taking place on all the islands, and each one had its own problems.

It was expected that in his official capacity Lord Saire should help them in every way he could, and he found that at Singapore alone there was an enormous amount of people wishing to see him.

They all had complaints that he was expected to convey to the British Government.

There was also an extensive programme of official functions at which he was expected to be present.

But he swept all this aside with an imperious wave of his hand, saying that before he did anything else he wished to be conveyed to Sarawak.

He was too used to getting his own way, especially where officials were concerned, for there to be any real opposition.

It was only a question of time before he could go aboard the gun-boat and feel with a sense of relief that at last he was able to follow Bertilla.

He had deliberately been careful not to let anyone know the real object of his visit, so as to ensure that Bertilla was not gossiped about by the women he most disliked.

As she had suffered from that already, he had no intention of subjecting her to it again.

He therefore on arrival at Kuching arranged that the ship should anchor close to the steps which led to the Astana Palace.

The arrival of a gun-boat was an event of great excitement. The crowds tore down to the riverside, and long before the ship let down its anchor the banks were lined with people.

Several officials were there to meet Lord Saire and to escort him and the Captain of the gun-boat into the Palace.

The exterior of the building was long and white with sloping roofs and a great stone baronic tower where a sentry was always on guard.

Inside there were enormous rooms stretching the whole length, which were, Lord Saire was amused to note, a fantastic medley of beauty and bad taste.

There was, Lord Saire thought, nothing wrong with their proportions, but the Rajah had filled them with an appalling confusion of reproduction furniture from every period of English and French history.

Early Victorian mahogany was arranged stiffly against the walls, mirrors were dotted about on tin-legged tables, and Dresden figures held caskets in their chipped and broken hands.

At a glance, Lord Saire realised however that the ceilings were beautiful.

Heavily carved with gorgeous dragons and flowers of plain plaster, they had been designed and executed by Chinese workmen.

He however had little time to look round before the White Rajah, Sir Charles Brooke, received him.

He was certainly a very distinguished-looking man with heavy white moustaches and curly grey hair above a high forehead.

He also had prominent white eye-brows, bags beneath his eyes, a wrinkled, turtle-like neck, and a bulky cleft jaw.

But his haughty expression, his cold austerity

to everyone with whom he had dealings, was that of a man who makes his own rules and expects everybody to comply with them.

Like Bertilla, Lord Saire had already been told that the White Rajah had a passion for the French.

He was steeped in the glamour of Napoleon and knew all his campaigns by heart.

He had little faith in the English newspapers, and his knowledge of world politics was based on his careful reading of *Le Figaro*, which he received when it was four or five weeks old.

To get into the White Rajah's good graces Lord Saire with his usual diplomatic skill had brought with him as a special present two books recently published in France.

One described Napoleon's battles, and the other was an expansive description of the addition of some new pictures to the Louvre.

He had been fortunate enough to buy one of them in Singapore and to purloin the other from the Governor's secretary the moment it arrived in a consignment of books from Europe.

The Rajah was delighted, and he spoke to Lord Saire in not quite such a dictatorial way as he addressed other people.

Lady Brooke had been beautiful in her youth and adored gaiety but she had suffered a great tragedy in her life.

Her first three children, a girl and twin boys, returning to England on the P. & O. steamer *Hydaspes* in 1873 had all died within a few hours of one another.

One day they were quite well, the next they were gasping for breath in the heat of the Red Sea.

No-one knew for certain what had caused their deaths, cholera, heat-stroke, a tin of poisoned milk — all were suggested later.

The children were buried at sea and for the rest of his life the Rajah avoided travelling on P. & O. steamers.

With fantastic courage the Ranee had returned to Sarawak and started a new family.

She had a dull, lonely life with a husband who worked to a time-table, who never listened to her opinions, and who never took her advice. She was never allowed to dance with another man nor to wear low-cut dresses.

Lord Saire charmed her with his good manners and his considerate attention from the first moment they met.

That evening as they sat at dinner in the great Dining-Room lit by hanging oil-lamps with Dyaks waving palm-leaves beside each guest, the table laid with silver and crystal, Lord Saire found it hard to believe he was on an isolated, barbaric island.

The Rajah was wearing his green and gold uniform, his chest blazing with decorations.

Everyone in the European community had been invited to meet Lord Saire and all the officers from the gun-boat were present.

Lord Saire noticed that the Rajah had arranged for the best-looking woman present to sit at his side.

He had spoken about women to Lord Saire before they went into dinner and confided as one man to another:

"A beautiful woman, a thoroughbred horse, and a well-designed yacht are the greatest joys in life."

Lord Saire agreed and was quite certain that the Rajah never deprived himself of any of those joys.

It was when dinner was over and Lord Saire was sitting beside the Ranee that he found the opportunity of speaking about what was uppermost in his mind.

"I hear you have a Missionary here in Sarawak," he said, "called Miss Agatha Alvinston."

The Ranee held up her hands as if in dismay.

"We have indeed, Lord Saire! A most tiresome woman! I cannot tell you the trouble she causes my poor husband one way or another. But how could you have heard about her?"

"Her sister-in-law, Lady Alvinston, is a frequent guest at Marlborough House."

"Oh, of course! I had forgotten," the Ranee said. "But then, I am sadly out of touch with the social life in England. You must tell me about it."

"Lady Alvinston is very beautiful."

"Which is something you cannot say about her sister-in-law. She is a most hideous woman, and I cannot help thinking as the years pass that she is growing a little mad."

"Mad?" Lord Saire questioned.

"She does such outrageous things and one hears very unpleasant tales about her treatment of the Mission children."

The Ranee sighed.

"I only wish Missionaries would leave the Dyaks alone. They are sweet and gentle if left to themselves and my husband has made so many improvements."

She saw the question in Lord Saire's eyes and laughed.

"Yes, they still head-hunt to a certain extent, but it is not half as prevalent as it was, and the pirates — the Sea Dyaks — have really behaved extremely well this last year. And that, I know, is one of the things which you will be investigating, Lord Saire."

"Of course," he agreed.

But, determined not to be side-tracked from what he wished to say, he went on:

"I do not know if you are aware of it, but Lady Alvinston's daughter has come out to Sarawak to stay with her aunt."

"Good heavens!" the Ranee exclaimed. "So that is who it was! I was told that a white girl had arrived on the steamer at the beginning of the week!"

She made a gesture with her fan and continued:

"I had expected her to be staying with one or another of our European community, but they are all here tonight, and when they did not ask to bring a guest with them, I realised I must have been wrong."

"Miss Alvinston was on the *Coromandel* with me," Lord Saire explained.

"Oh, the poor child! She must have been terrified by the fire! But I hear that everyone was rescued."

"We were indeed fortunate that it happened in the Malacca Straits," Lord Saire replied. "It might have been a very different story if it had occurred in the Red Sea."

He saw a shudder pass over the Ranee's face and realised he had been tactless.

"I suppose I ought to let Lady Alvinston know that her daughter is safe," he said quickly, "and I wanted to ask you how she was settling down with her aunt."

"I am sorry that I cannot answer that question," the Ranee replied, "but I will certainly visit the Mission first thing in the morning and meet Miss Alvinston."

She paused before she added:

"I am rather surprised at Lady Alvinston sending her here to her sister-in-law, but perhaps the girl will not be staying long."

"I think that is something we could discover tomorrow," Lord Saire said lightly.

He had got what he wanted and therefore turned the conversation to other matters.

As the Rajah rose at five o'clock in the morning to the sound of a single gun from the Fort, he did not like his guests to stay late at night.

The European community, having enjoyed enormously the party, which was an excitement in their monotonous lives, reluctantly rose to make their farewells.

They were all extremely effusive to Lord Saire, who promised to visit their plantations if he had time.

He knew that the idea of entertaining him put their wives into a flutter of anxiety in case their hospitality was not good enough for him.

He tried to reassure them by asserting that he was willing to take "pot-luck" and that they must not arrange anything for him, although he was quite certain that what he was saying fell on deaf ears.

Finally everybody had left except for the Captain, who was just about to return to his ship when one of the servants came hurrying into the huge Reception-Room to whisper in what seemed an agitated manner in the Rajah's ear.

He listened, then said in a voice of thunder:

"It is all that damned woman's fault! She deserves anything that happens to her!"

"What has occurred?" the Ranee asked.

The Rajah's eyes were angry under his beetling white eye-brows as he answered:

"I am told that the Dyaks are attacking the Mission House. I suppose that means I shall have to send my soldiers to save that tiresome, idiotic woman from the retribution she has brought upon her own head."

"Attacking the Mission House?" Lord Saire exclaimed. "Then I would like, Sir, if I may, to go with them, and surely we should move as quickly as possible?"

Urged on by Lord Saire, it was only a few

minutes before a number of soldiers in their white uniforms with black-and-red headdresses were on the way from the Palace along the road which led to the Mission.

Lord Saire and the Captain of the gun-boat went with them, and as they neared the clearing they heard the sound of gun-shots.

The officer in charge of the soldiers said to Lord Saire, who was marching along beside him:

"That'll be the old lady. She's quite a dab hand with a gun and has killed or wounded quite a number of Dyaks who have interfered with her in the past."

Although Lord Saire could not see his face, he knew that the man was grinning, finding Agatha Alvinston's resistance amusing.

But he himself was afraid for Bertilla — more afraid than he had ever been before. He had not believed it possible that he could feel so desperate about anyone.

How, he asked himself furiously, could he have allowed her, knowing what he knew about Sarawak, to come out here alone and unprotected, and stay with an aunt whom everybody had disparaged and spoken of with contempt?

He thought of how soft and gentle she had been when he held her in his arms.

As he remembered the ecstasy they both felt when his lips had touched hers, he thought that if anything happened to Bertilla through his own crass stupidity he would no longer wish to go on living.

It was an emotional response that would have been utterly and completely inconceivable to him a few weeks ago.

Yet he knew in his despair that he was terrified that he might be too late, and that when he reached the Mission House he would find Bertilla decapitated.

He thought he would go mad as the road through the jungle seemed endless, the movement of the troops so slow that he wanted to cry out with frustration.

His feeling of anxiety made him so tense and on edge that it was hard for him to control his voice and reply naturally when he was spoken to.

"Bertilla! Bertilla!"

His whole being was crying out to her, and he knew that it was only a question of time before the Dyaks, even though they were armed only with their sharp carved krisses, would close in and overpower one woman firing at them with one gun.

Agatha Alvinston was still firing when at last Lord Saire heard the officer giving the order to his men to charge.

It had been almost too dark to see as they marched beneath the trees whose branches met over the road, forming a leafy tunnel through which the moonlight could not percolate.

But now the Mission House could be seen as clear as daylight and as they burst in on the children's playground, Lord Saire saw the Dyaks run away from them back into the jungle.

There was no mistaking that they were carrying their war-weapons and wearing helmets of short, tufted feathers on their heads.

He saw the moonlight glinting on their shields and on their curved krisses.

Then as they vanished among the trees and there was only the rattle of soldiers' guns as they fired after them, Lord Saire ran frantically towards what he saw now was the open door of the Mission.

He passed through it and saw lying on the ground the gun which Agatha Alvinston must have been using, and a number of empty cartridge cases were beside it.

But there was no sign of her and Lord Saire hurried towards the other part of the house.

The kitchen was empty and he felt as if an icy hand clutched at his heart.

He knew then that he had lost the one thing that mattered more to him than anything else in the world — Bertilla.

He tried to call her name, but his lips were dry and he made no sound.

Then he saw there was a closed door on the other side of the kitchen.

Without much hope he opened it, to see standing opposite him, her back pressed against the wall, an expression of absolute terror on her face, Bertilla!

In the light from the moon coming through the window, they stood staring at each other. Then with an inarticulate cry that was somehow infinitely pathetic she ran towards him.

He could not speak, he could not even kiss her hair as it touched his lips.

He only knew as he held her against him that his whole heart, mind, and soul were singing with the knowledge that what he had feared had not happened.

Bertilla was alive!

Chapter Seven

Bertilla was trembling in Lord Saire's arms. Then at length she said in an inarticulate whisper he could hardly hear:

"I was . . . frightened . . . I h-hid under the bed . . . and I was praying . . . that you would s-save me."

"You knew I was here in Sarawak?" he asked, his voice unsteady.

"N-no . . . but I thought of you and I . . . tried to tell you . . . wherever you were, how f-frightened I was."

"I have saved you, Bertilla," he said, "and it is all over. There is nothing now to make you afraid."

He felt her relax against him as the tension went out of her body, and now he raised his head to look at the moonlight on her hair, and her eyes turned up to his.

"It is all right," he said again, and knew that while her hands still clung to his coat she was not as terrified as she had been.

There was the sound of a step behind them,

and the officer in charge of the soldiers said:

"I was looking for you, M'Lord."

"I have found Miss Bertilla," Lord Saire replied.

There was a note of triumph in his voice almost as if he had scaled a high mountain or swum a deep river.

"Could I speak to you a moment, M'Lord?"

Lord Saire looked down at Bertilla and her hands tightened on him as if she was afraid to lose him.

"Sit down on your bed for a moment," he said gently. "I will not go out of your sight, so there is no need to be afraid. I have brought soldiers with me and all the Dyaks have run away."

He knew it was with a superhuman effort at self-control that Bertilla said nothing and allowed him to help her to the bed. She sat down on the edge of it.

As she did so he noticed for the first time the poverty and discomfort of the room and felt furious that Bertilla should have been made to suffer such hardships quite unnecessarily.

Then he smiled at her reassuringly and walked out of the room and into the kitchen, leaving the door open so that she could see him and not feel that she had been left alone.

The officer spoke in a very low voice.

"There is no sign of Miss Agatha Alvinston, M'Lord, but there are trails of blood going into the jungle, which may be hers, or it may have come from a Dyak she had wounded."

The officer paused, and added a little uncomfortably:

"My men are not anxious to search until it is daylight."

Lord Saire understood that.

He knew that the Dyaks were past-masters at hiding until their victim had almost passed them, then lopping off his head with a single stroke of a kriss.

"I am sure it would be wise to leave everything until the morning," he said, and saw the relief in the officer's face.

"What about the young lady, M'Lord?"

"We will take Miss Bertilla Alvinston back with us to the Palace," Lord Saire said firmly. "Is there anyway of getting a conveyance of some sort? It would be rather a long walk for her."

"I will send for one immediately," the officer said.

"That would be excellent," Lord Saire agreed, "but I would rather you and your men guarded us until we are actually able to leave the Mission."

"Of course, M'Lord."

Lord Saire looked round the kitchen and saw a pair of candlesticks on a table.

The officer followed the direction of his eyes and hurried to light the candles.

The moonlight was so brilliant that it was easy to see without them. At the same time, Lord Saire thought they would somehow reassure Bertilla.

The golden light dispersed the shadows and seemed to make everything less frightening.

It revealed, somehow, even more than in Bertilla's bed-room, the poverty and the primitive discomfort of the kitchen and even the poor quality of the cooking-utensils.

Lord Saire said nothing but his lips tightened.

As the officer moved away to give orders to his men, he went back into the bed-room to sit down beside Bertilla and put his arms round her.

"I am taking you to stay at the Palace with the Rajah and Lady Brooke," he said. "They will look after you, as I should have done."

She looked up at him enquiringly, her eyes very large in her pale face, and yet he saw that the terror had gone from them and once again she was trusting him.

"I am really very angry with you for running away from the Hendersons without saying good-bye to me," he said, but his voice was soft and gentle.

She looked away from him towards the moon-light outside.

"I know why you went," Lord Saire said, "but it was quite unnecessary. That is something I want to talk to you about when we have more time and certainly in more comfortable circumstances."

She did not reply and after a moment he said in a different tone of voice:

"As you will not be coming back here, I suggest you pack your clothes and we will take them with us to the Palace."

"I have only unpacked part of one trunk,"

Bertilla said. "There was so little space to put anything."

Lord Saire saw that her trunks were in fact standing in a corner of her room.

Bertilla rose from the bed, took a few garments from a very dilapidated chest-of-drawers, and lifted down two gowns from the hooks on which they were hanging on the wall.

It took her less than five minutes to add to the trunk her brushes and comb and a pair of slippers that were under the bed.

Lord Saire, very much at his ease, sat watching her.

He thought how sweet and unselfconscious she was and that she moved with a grace that reminded him of a gazelle.

Finally she looked round and said:

"I think that is everything. I would not wish to leave behind any of the lovely things which Mrs. Henderson gave me."

She shut the top of her round-topped leather trunk as she spoke and Lord Saire rose to say:

"Leave it. I will get the soldiers to strap it up for you and bring it outside. I imagine it will not be long now before a conveyance arrives to take us to the Palace."

He was right in that assumption, for by the time they reached the open door at the front of the Mission House a carriage drawn by two horses was coming towards them.

The soldiers piled the trunks on the back. Then, having helped Bertilla into the open carriage, Lord Saire sat beside her and as the horses started off took her hand in his.

"You are no longer frightened?" he asked.

"Not now . . . you are here."

Then in a low voice she asked:

"What has . . . happened to Aunt Agatha?"

He knew that the question had been in her mind ever since he'd arrived and he was glad he could answer truthfully when he said:

"I have no idea. She may have run into the jungle or the Dyaks may have taken her with them, but there is nothing the soldiers can do until the morning."

"I was afraid that . . . something like this would . . . happen," Bertilla said in a low voice, "when I saw a Dyak watching her . . . beat one of the women so . . . unmercifully."

"Your aunt beat her?" Lord Saire asked in amazement.

"She was always . . . beating the women who were supposed to help her . . . teach the children and were sent to the Mission instead of having to go to . . . prison."

Lord Saire said nothing, but he could understand only too well that the Dyaks would resent one of their women, whatever crime she might have committed, being ill-treated by a Missionary for whom they had little respect.

His fingers tightened on Bertilla's hand.

"Forget what has happened for tonight, Bertilla," he said. "We can talk about it tomorrow."

Bertilla turned towards him with a child-like gesture and hid her face against his shoulder.

"I . . . I think Aunt Agatha is . . . d-dead," she said, "and although it is . . . wrong of me . . . I cannot be very unhappy about it. I think she had gone a little mad."

"Do not think about it tonight," Lord Saire admonished.

A moment later they saw just ahead of them the lighted windows of the Astana Palace, and then they were passing through the well-kept gardens surrounding it.

Lord Saire knew that Bertilla was nervous as they stepped out at the front door.

But when the Ranee with a smile of welcome kissed her, he knew she was in good hands.

Bertilla lay on a *chaise longue* in the garden and looked at the butterflies hovering over the flowers, some of them almost as large as small birds.

Their wings were covered with peacock-coloured blue-green scales that shimmered and gleamed in the sun.

She felt as if they symbolised the thoughts that shone within her mind and were so beautiful that she dared not put a name to them.

She had on the Ranee's orders not been called until late in the morning.

When she was dressed she had come downstairs to be told that a *chaise longue* was waiting for her in the garden and that Lord Saire had gone out with the Rajah but would be seeing her later.

A servant had brought her a cool drink and she lay in the shade of a tree heavy with blossoms.

As she looked at the orchids and other flowers growing so profusely round her, she felt that she had stepped into Paradise.

She could hardly believe it was possible that Lord Saire had actually appeared in answer to her prayers and saved her as she had longed for him to do.

She had been panic-stricken when as night fell and the moon came out she was aware that there were movements among the trees outside the Mission House and they were not caused by the wind.

There was no dusk in Sarawak and darkness came swiftly like a veil falling over the land.

Then there was the brilliance of the stars and the clear, silver light of the moon to illuminate everything, and yet at the same time it made the shadows seem ominous.

The slightest movement could create terror!

All day long her aunt had been more unbearable than ever, screaming at the women and singling out the Dyak woman for special abuse.

She had not actually beaten her again, as if she knew she had gone too far the day before.

But she had threatened her and she had beaten the others and several of the children until the whole place seemed to be filled with the noise of their screaming.

To Bertilla it was all horrifying and several times during the day she had run to her room to shut the door and fling herself down on her bed.

She had put her hands over her ears so that she could no longer hear the cries of those who were being hurt.

Her aunt had called her and she had to go back to help with the children, to tidy up after they had gone, and to cook a meagre meal for her and her aunt to eat in the primitive kitchen.

There was very little, so what there was was soon finished. Then Bertilla had gone to the window to look out at the night.

She hoped its beauty would erase from her mind the sordid scenes she had been forced to witness that day. But as she stood there she had seen the bushes move.

At first she thought it was some animal or perhaps one of the larger hornbills which she was still hoping to see.

But the leaves were moving not only in one place but all round the mud compound.

Now Bertilla felt that she was waiting, and it was hard to breathe because she had begun to be afraid of what she might see.

There was another movement and this time she had a glimpse of what she was sure were the short plumes which the Dyak men wore on their heads.

"Aunt Agatha!" she had cried, an urgent note in her voice.

"What is it?" her aunt enquired.

"There are men out there. They are hiding, but I am sure I can see them."

Her aunt had jumped to her feet to come to the window.

Then she had made a sound that was almost one of elation, and to Bertilla's surprise she had reached out to close the wooden shutters with a slam.

"I will teach them! I will show them!" she mumbled. "Coming here to threaten me as they have done before!"

"Who has threatened you? Who are they?" Bertilla asked.

But her aunt was already pulling a gun out of a cupboard and carrying it with a box of cartridges into the Class-Room.

Bertilla had put the shutters over the windows after she had cleaned the rooms, not that she had thought at the time to keep people out, but to prevent the insects with which the forest abounded from coming.

There were not only moths and beetles but bats and small birds which would fly all over the place unless kept out.

Her aunt was still talking to herself:

"They will get more than they bargained for — I will teach them a lesson they will not forget. Barbarians! Savages! Murderers! If I kill two or three of them they will soon learn who is the master!"

Bertilla watched her in perplexity as she knelt down in front of one of the shuttered windows, then removed a small piece of wood from the lower part of it.

It made an aperture through which she could poke her gun, and now having loaded it she knelt down, looked down the barrel, and fired.

The explosion made Bertilla jump and the noise seemed to echo and reecho round the room.

Then from the outside there was a shrill cry and Bertilla ran to her aunt's side.

"You have shot someone! Oh, Aunt Agatha, you cannot do this! You have shot someone and you may have killed him!"

"Go and hide yourself, you little coward!" her aunt said harshly.

Because there was something so contemptuous in the way she spoke, Bertilla took a few steps backwards.

Suddenly frightened not only by what was outside but also by her aunt's behaviour, she ran back into the kitchen.

She stood irresolute, then realised that although the shutters were closed it was not dark because they fitted so badly.

There were spaces between the flat boards, through which the moonlight was percolating.

Hardly aware of what she was doing, she went close to the window to look out through an aperture to see what was happening outside.

Then she gave a cry of sheer horror, for advancing from the protection of the trees she could see a dozen Dyaks and she knew at once what they intended.

There was no mistaking their war-dress, the feathers on their heads and shoulders, and the tufts of hair on their shields.

Each one carried a curved kriss and the sharp steel glinted evilly in the light from the moon.

She could see very clearly the elephants' teeth in their ears and the blue tattoos on their arms.

Their long black hair hung almost to their waists and it seemed to Bertilla there was a ferocious expression on their faces that could not be misunderstood.

Now her aunt was firing at them, and while they were obviously nervous of the bullets, they did not retreat but moved from tree to tree, occasionally coming out onto the compound, then moving back again.

They were making it appear almost like a childish game, but at the same time Bertilla was well aware they were manoeuvring for position.

Then one Dyak uttered a sound that was like a whoop of defiance and aggression — a war-cry — and as he did so he slashed the air with his kriss.

All the other men wielded theirs in the same way, making the blades cut through the air, and it was only too clear what would happen.

Bertilla cried out in terror.

She ran away from the window to rush into her bed-room and creep under the bed, thinking it was the only protection she could find.

Then she had prayed — prayed for Lord Saire to save her as he had done before.

Her prayers were incoherent and the words tumbled over themselves, but in her heart she cried out to him desperately, despairingly, like a frightened child.

Last night after the Ranee, sweet and motherly as her own mother had never been, had left her, Bertilla before going to sleep had thanked God.

She thanked Him for sending Lord Saire to her rescue and for saving her from being decapitated by the Dyaks.

She had thought as she crouched beneath her bed that at any moment she might find herself pulled out from under it, perhaps by her hair.

Then the last thing she would hear in her life would be the swish of the kriss as it fell to sever her head from her body.

But miraculously she had escaped!

Now as Lord Saire came towards her, walking across the lawn between the flowers, she thought for a moment that he was wearing the shining armour of a Knight and that he held in his hand the spear with which he had killed the dragon.

He was smiling as he reached her, and as impulsively she held out both her hands to his he took them and kissed first one, then the other.

"You slept well?" he asked in his deep voice.

Because he had kissed her hands Bertilla was blushing and could not look at him, but after a moment she replied:

"Lady Brooke must have given me . . . something to make me sleep . . . and whatever it was, when I awoke . . . it was disgracefully late!"

"And you are not too tired?"

She shook her head. Then because she knew it

was the question she must ask, she said in a low voice:

"You have . . . heard about Aunt . . . Agatha?"

Lord Saire sat down on the edge of the couch and kept both her hands in his.

"I am afraid I cannot bring you any good news."

"She is . . . dead?"

"Yes, Bertilla. She is dead. I do not think she suffered — not for long at any rate."

He had no intention of telling Bertilla the details of how the soldiers searching the jungle round the Mission House early this morning had found Miss Alvinston's body.

The Dyaks must have carried her off with them when, having broken down the Mission door, they heard the soldiers running and retreated into the jungle.

Her body had been found lying on the track that their feet had made beneath the trees.

They had taken nothing from her pockets nor even removed the cameo brooch she always wore at the neck of her gown — but her head was missing.

It was what was to be expected, Lord Saire thought. But there was no need for Bertilla to know anything except that her aunt was dead.

She did not speak for a moment. Then as if she knew that he did not wish to discuss it further, she said:

"Why . . . are you here? You said you might come to Sarawak, and I was so hoping you would do so . . . but I did not expect you so . . . soon."

Lord Saire smiled, then he released her hands.

"That is what I want to talk to you about."

She looked at him questioningly, and after a moment he said:

"When you left the Hendersons' home with such unnecessary haste, I knew there was only one thing I could do — and that was to follow you."

Still she did not answer, but he saw the colour rise in her cheeks.

"You see, darling," he said very softly, "I realised when you were gone that I could not live without you."

She looked at him incredulously.

"It is true," he said as if she had asked the question. "I love you, Bertilla. I need you and want you as I have never wanted anyone before in all my life."

There was a light in her eyes that seemed to come from within her and it illuminated her whole face.

In a whisper that he could hardly hear she said:

"I . . . think I must be . . . dreaming."

"It is no dream," he answered, "it is fact. I love you, my darling, and we will be married as soon as it can be arranged."

She held her breath in sheer astonishment at his words. Then Lord Saire bent forward, put his arms round her, and his lips were on hers.

He kissed her and as he did so he wondered if it would be possible for any kiss to be as wonderful as it had been the first time their lips met.

Then as he felt Bertilla's mouth soft beneath

his, as her hands fluttered towards him almost like the movement of a butterfly and her whole body seemed to vibrate to his touch, he knew once again that incredible ecstasy.

It joined them as it had before, only now it was even more intense and more wonderful.

It was a long time before he took his lips from Bertilla's to say, his voice deep and moved:

"I love you, my precious heart, I love you! And this is the truth — I have never felt like this before in the whole of my life."

She gave a little cry that was half a sob before she whispered:

"I love you, I have loved you. I think, from the first moment I saw you, but I never thought . . . never imagined that you would love me."

"We belong to each other," Lord Saire said.

Then he was kissing her again, frantically, wildly, passionately, until her body moved against him and her eyes seemed to hold all the sunlight there was in the garden.

It was a long time later that the intensity of their feelings for each other allowed the laughter to come back into Lord Saire's voice.

"You know, my darling, that I am called the Love Pirate," he said. "Well, let me tell you that this pirate has struck his flag and he will no longer roam the seas. He has found the treasure he always sought and he is utterly and completely content."

"How can you be sure . . . I will be . . . enough

for you after all the . . . beautiful, clever women you have . . . known?" Bertilla asked, her face hidden against his shoulder.

"They always disappointed me," he said frankly, "and through the years I have grown very disillusioned. That is why I intended never to marry."

She looked tip at him swiftly and he saw a sudden fear in her eyes.

"Until I met you," he smiled, "then I knew, although not at once, that you were the ideal I had kept hidden in my heart but never thought to find."

"You are so . . . magnificent . . . so important," Bertilla said. "I am . . . afraid I might fail you."

"You could only do that if you did not love me enough."

"It would be . . . impossible for me not to . . . love you," she whispered.

"That is all I ask for in the future," Lord Saire said, "that we should be together to discover and develop our love for each other until there is nothing else of any consequence in our lives."

"There has never been anything of . . . consequence for me except . . . you," Bertilla said passionately. "I knew when you were so kind to me on the station that you were someone I had dreamt of but thought never to meet."

"And I was certain that you did not exist except in my imagination," Lord Saire replied. "But you do, and, my darling, I cannot imagine anyone could be more perfect, more lovely in every way, not only in your exquisite little face but also inside, in your heart and in your mind."

As he spoke, he thought that that was what had always been missing before — an inner loveliness which was spiritual and without which no woman could be really beautiful.

He put his fingers under her chin and turned her face up to his, looking at her searchingly.

Bertilla blushed.

"You are making me . . . shy," she protested.

"I adore you shy," he answered, "but I am looking to see why you are so lovely."

"Do not look too closely . . . and find all the . . . flaws."

"Are there any? I love your honest, worried eyes, and never again will I see fear in them."

Lord Saire kissed her eyes before he went on:

"I am entranced by your small straight nose, but most of all I am held captive by your lips."

Bertilla waited for him to kiss her, but he moved his fingers lightly over the outline of her mouth.

It made her thrill in a strange way and as he felt her quiver and saw the colour rise in her cheeks he laughed very tenderly.

"My precious darling, I have so much to teach you."

"There is so . . . much I want to learn," Bertilla replied. "Please . . . please . . . make me do all the things you . . . want, and which will make . . . you happy."

He kissed her with a passion that left her breathless and pulsating in his arms.

"I have a suggestion to make," he said at length.

"What is that?" she asked.

"You are officially in mourning, my sweet little love, and even though I think it would be hypocritical for you to mourn your aunt, if we are married immediately in Singapore it might make people think you are somewhat heartless."

Bertilla looked at him apprehensively as he went on:

"I am therefore going to suggest, if you will agree, that we be married by the Captain of the gun-boat which brought me here yesterday."

He saw the excitement spring into Bertilla's eyes as she asked, almost stammering with sheer joy:

"C-can we . . . really . . . do that?"

"It is perfectly legal: every Captain of a ship can, by the power vested in him by the Queen, marry anyone at sea."

"Then let us be . . . married like that . . . if you are sure . . . really sure that you wish to marry someone as . . . unimportant as I."

"You are very, very important and very precious as far as I am concerned," Lord Saire said, "and I thought, if you agree, once we are married we will continue together my visits to the islands."

He paused to say, as if he had just thought of it:

"We can travel in the gun-boat, and perhaps in a month or two, maybe longer, return to Singapore."

"It sounds too wonderful . . . too perfect! I cannot find words in which to tell you what it would . . . mean to me."

"It will be a somewhat unusual honeymoon," Lord Saire said, "but we can make arrangements at every place at which we stop for them to allow us some days off, and I am quite certain there will be people willing to lend us a house where we can be alone."

"Now I know I am dreaming!" Bertilla cried. "To be in this unbelievably beautiful part of the world and to be with you . . . this could never happen in . . . real life."

"It is happening," Lord Saire said.

He kissed her until his lips gave her sensations she had never known existed and she wanted him to go on touching her in a way which in her innocence she did not understand.

They had forgotten time and everything else when a servant came to tell them that the Rajah was waiting for them to join him for luncheon.

Lord Saire rose from the *chaise longue* to say:

"Shall we tell them what we have decided?"

"I shall feel . . . embarrassed," Bertilla answered.

"Leave everything to me," Lord Saire commanded.

"That is . . . what I want to do," she told him. "I have been so afraid and so lonely, and this last week I have been wondering who I could talk to and tell them that I thought Aunt Agatha was going a little mad!"

She gave a deep sigh and went on:

"But no-one came to the Mission and there

was no-one there except my aunt who could speak English."

He knew by her voice what she had suffered, and as the servant had gone ahead of them he put his arms round her as they stood out of sight behind a great bush of crimson and white rhododendrons.

"You will never be alone again," he vowed. "I should never have left you, never let you out of my sight, but I promise you in the future we will always be together."

"I love you!" Bertilla answered. "I love you until I feel as if I was . . . made of love, that everything I am is yours, completely and absolutely."

"That is what I want," he answered.

Then he pulled her into his arms and kissed her until the garden seemed to whirl round her.

The colours, the scent of the flowers, and the flight of the butterflies seemed to mingle with the love which filled her heart and mind until she became a part of him and they were indivisible.

There was only love — a love that was part of the Divine, sacred and unspoilt, true and faithful between one man and one woman now and for all eternity.

"I love you! God, how much I love you!" Lord Saire said hoarsely.

Faintly against his lips Bertilla echoed his words:

"I love you . . . I love you with . . . all of me!"